BIBI BLUNDERMUSS

and the TREE ACROSS the COSMOS

ANDREW DURKIN

YeLLow
BiKe
— PRESS —

Published by Yellow Bike Press, Portland, Oregon
yellowbikepress.com

Cover and interior art by Devin Watson

First edition
Paperback ISBN 978-0-578-97206-0

For anyone trying to find the courage

PART ONE
THE SAPLING

CHAPTER ONE:
The Girl Who Was Scared of Trees

"Leave me alone!" Bibi Blundermuss cried, twisting in her sleep and kicking a dictionary-size book off the edge of her mattress. It landed on the wooden floor with a *slap*.

Bibi snapped upright in the drape-darkened bedroom, breathing hard and fast. She swatted her tangled brown hair out of her eyes, listening to the howl of the wind as it leaned into the house. Her whole body ached, as if she had truly been fleeing from the trees—not just dreaming about it.

"Another nightmare," she said. "Not real." Listening to her breath, she tried to slow it down. *Inhale. Exhale.* That helped, a little. She waited for her heartbeat to return to normal, and for the sweat to evaporate from her palms.

As always, her memory of the nightmare was hazy—obscured, as if behind white mist. She remembered the trees—

trees that moved, chasing her with clawlike branches, which opened and closed with a *tok, tok, tok*. But the other details faded fast, as if drawn in disappearing ink. The more Bibi worked to remember, the quicker they vanished.

She squinted around the room, listening to the lonely wind, and hoping to see her little black cat somewhere in the gloom. She tried her usual greeting, the Zulu word for "hello."

"*Sawubona*, Eek?"

Eek's usual response—"*Sawubona*, Bibi!"—didn't come.

Where was she? Bibi put on her green-rimmed glasses. "*Sawubona*, Eek?" she said again, louder, trying to ignore the groans of the real trees as they swayed in the wind outside. She shivered and got out of bed, putting on her green T-shirt and jeans, her smartphone heavy in the pocket. She stumbled over to the door and peeked down the murky hallway—first one side, then the other.

"*Sawubona*, Eek?" she said.

No cat. No anyone. Bibi frowned. Had Eek already gone downstairs?

She went back to the bedroom. The book she had kicked out of bed still lay on the floor. Bibi squatted, tracing a finger along one worn edge. She stared at the title—*An Encyclopedia of Fear*—printed in embossed red letters. *Not the best book for a twelve-year-old*, Ms. MacTavish had said, but Bibi had checked it out anyway.

Picking the book up and carrying it into the adjoining bathroom, Bibi flipped on the fluorescent light with an elbow. She set the book on the counter—next to the bottle of anti-anxiety pills she was supposed to take whenever leaving the house.

The pills. She made a face and pushed them away. She knew the right ones would help, but these didn't. Not without making her forget things. She'd ask for a better kind, next appointment.

Brushing her teeth, Bibi flipped through the book's pages. "*Haphephobia*," she read aloud through a mouthful of toothpaste, unsure how to pronounce the word. "The fear of being touched. *Heliophobia*, the fear of the sun. *Hippophobia*, the fear of horses."

Weird fears, all right—but not as weird as hers. She thought of the whispers she had heard in her school's hallways. Mostly from Ellery Finley, or one of the other eighth-graders. *You won't believe what she's scared of.* She bit down on her toothbrush, cheeks going red.

After spitting and rinsing, Bibi wiped her mouth and hands.

"*Hylophobia*," she said when she found the passage, marked with a Post-It. "The fear of trees or forests. Often beginning in nightmares."

Ugh. Her nightmares had started six months ago. After she moved to this woodland house with her mom and dad. After they vanished. Bibi thought the nightmares had something to do with the forest that began just beyond the side door and went on for miles. Why had her parents wanted to move here? Bibi had been happy back in Portland. Now her parents were gone, and she was scared to death of the stupid trees.

The wind sent twigs and debris skittering across the roof. Bibi looked up, bit her lip. *Inhale. Exhale.* Furrowing her brow, she returned her gaze to the book.

"Sometimes prompted by the mere sight of a tree," she continued, "and made worse by physical contact with one, hylophobia is a rare condition that is poorly understood. It progresses through a range of symptoms—beginning in nausea, and moving to dizziness, seizures, and ultimately a comatose state—"

Bbbrrriiinnnggg!

Bibi jumped, slamming the book shut as the sound of the old-fashioned downstairs phone cut through the howl of the wind. *You won't believe what she's scared of.* She would stay inside today, with Eek and Grandma Ivy—shades down and curtains closed, to keep out the sight of the forest. It was Saturday, after all. *Breathe.*

The ringing continued, and Bibi turned off the bathroom light, scrambling to the bedroom door. "Grandma *Ivy!*" she called. "*Phone!*"

Clutching the book to her chest as a shield, she headed downstairs.

CHAPTER TWO:
Tons of Honey

Bbbrrriiinnnggg!

Bibi leapt down the long dark staircase, two steps at a time. The wind wailed louder—like a sky full of ghosts. It would be good to be downstairs, with her grandma and cat. She tried not to think of the trees swaying outside.

Bbbrrriiinnnggg!

"Okay, okay!" Bibi reached the first floor at last, catching her breath in the empty hallway next to the kitchen, and moving toward the old-fashioned phone, mounted on the wall. Why did people even use those anymore? Tucking *An Encyclopedia of Fear* under one arm, she lifted the receiver and pressed it to her ear. "Hello?"

"*Sawubona*, Bibi," said a sweet old voice on the other end.

"Grandma *Ivy?*" The voice surprised Bibi so much that she almost dropped her book. "Where are you?"

The line crackled with static, mixed with the jangle of Grandma Ivy's bracelets. "Why, I have Garden Club today. Don't you remember?"

Of course. Every first Saturday of the month, from nine to noon, in Pine Ridge—thirty minutes away. Bibi opened her mouth to respond, but her nose suddenly itched, and she paused to scratch it.

"I'm calling to make sure you take your pill this morning, dear," Grandma Ivy said. "I won't be back 'til later. You should take it first thing, with food."

A gust of wind slammed into the house, making the shutters clatter. Bibi's nose itched again, and she caught a whiff of something strong and sweet in the air. She paused, sniffing deep. Honey.

Huh? She sniffed again. Yes, definitely honey. But not from a jar—*wild* honey, like in a field of flowers. She pursed her lips.

"Bibi?" Grandma Ivy said.

"Um—not yet, but I will." Bibi cradled the phone between her ear and shoulder, so she could scratch her nose some more. "Grandma Ivy, did you *bake* something before you left this morning? Something sweet?" Grandma Ivy loved to bake. Maybe she'd been using the honey for muffins, or pancakes.

"No." Grandma Ivy rattled her bracelets again. "Why?"

The wind got heavier, and then eased off once more—as if being wildly adjusted with a dial.

Shifting her weight, Bibi switched the phone to her other

ear. "Because it smells like honey in here! Like tons of honey." The scent hung everywhere—so sweet that it almost burned the back of her throat. Where had it come from? Eek might know. In the kitchen, a feeble light burned bravely against the darkness of the gathering storm. The bowl of cat kibble hadn't been touched. Where *was* Eek, anyway?

"Perhaps you're hungry, dear," Grandma Ivy said. "Get yourself some breakfast—I left cereal and a bowl on the counter. And don't forget that pill! Now, I should go—"

"Wait!" Bibi said, standing a little straighter. "Grandma Ivy, have you seen Eek today?"

"Ekaterina? Let me think." Grandma Ivy paused. "Yes! She rose early. She asked to go outside, so I let her—"

"Out*side!*" Bibi said. "But the storm!"

As if on cue, the wind exploded—the strongest burst so far. The light in the kitchen dimmed, went out, came back on. Spurts of static erupted on the phone. Bibi could hardly hear her grandma at all.

"Storm? . . . *tzzzkt!* . . . my dear . . . *kzzzt!* . . . Ekaterina . . . *fzzttt!* . . . rose early—"

With a *click*, the connection went dead.

"Grandma Ivy? Grandma *Ivy?*" For a moment, Bibi stood, holding the silent receiver—dread pooling like bile in her belly.

Eek! Out in the storm!

She hung up the phone and dashed into the kitchen, where a weathered side door led into the yard. Eek's favorite way in and out of the house—and a mere stone's throw from the forest. Wide-eyed, Bibi watched the door jiggle in its frame.

9

She had to open it. She had to open it *right away*. She squeezed the book in her arms. The trees waited on the other side. But Eek did too. She must be desperate to come in from the storm. No time to go upstairs and get a pill. *Open the door. OPEN IT.*

Bibi clenched her teeth and turned the brass knob.

CHAPTER THREE:
A Runaway Game of Ping-Pong

A powerful gust whipped the door out of Bibi's hand, slamming it back against the kitchen wall. The wind pressed on her face, filling her nose with so much honey scent that she almost fainted from the sweetness.

Planting her feet, Bibi squeezed her book tighter to her chest, looking through scrunched eyelids at the stoop where Eek usually waited to come into the house.

Empty.

"Eek?" Bibi yelled, shielding her face against the onslaught of air as it tossed her hair in every direction. *Don't look at the trees.* Pressing a palm against one arm of her glasses so they wouldn't blow off, she stood in the door frame and squinted harder toward Eek's favorite haunts. The rose bushes. The clover patch next to the garage. The place where the driveway met the dirt road. All empty.

"Eek—where *are* you?"

A knot of clouds churned in the east. With rain coming, the wind screamed. The trees, which seemed to go on forever, leaned back and forth in unison, like faceless soldiers in formation. *Don't look at them. DON'T!*

Another sound began. A low, moaning hum. No—a buzz. Almost hidden at first under the noise of the wind, it grew steadily, like a badly-out-of-tune orchestra, playing the same note, louder every second.

Bees?

Bibi had seen a bee swarm once, in an open field near school. The insects had spread out with shimmering zig-zags, like sunlight reflected on a lake. But in a storm? How could bees fly in the wind? She swallowed hard, trying to get the harsh taste of too-sweet honey out of her throat.

Something on the right side of the yard caught her attention. A black blur. Tail high, it shot like an arrow across the driveway.

"Eek!"

Faster than Bibi could react, the little cat sprinted along the gray wooden fence that lined the forest. As she whizzed past the stoop, the buzzing grew—an ugly motorboat sound, so loud that it hurt Bibi's ears—coming from a much larger black blur, following Eek just as fast.

Bibi swallowed again. The swarm of bees!

"*EEK!*" she yelled, stepping onto the porch—then recoiling from the looming trees. The buzzing and the wind seemed to cut through her. Eek moved so fast—no sooner had she reached one end of the yard than she doubled back, the swarm trailing her like a hungry black hole.

Bibi waved her arms, trying to get Eek's attention. She jumped up and down. "Come in*side*, Eek! Over *here*, Eek!" But Eek zigzagged, and the bees zigzagged, left, right, left—like a runaway game of Ping-Pong.

At last, Eek faked one way, but went the other, scrambling under the gray gate and into the forest. Bibi's heart dropped. She tried to run after her cat—but her legs refused to move, as if chained to the porch. She could only watch as the swarm zoomed behind Eek, and both disappeared down the dark forest aisles.

Gone. *Gone!*

Bibi stood, shaking from head to toe, before the howling wind and towering trees. No, no, no—not the forest! She covered her face with her hands.

What could she do? The wind raged stronger, as if angered by her indecision—grabbing her by the shoulders and shaking, threatening to blow her away if she didn't take cover. It took all her strength to duck back into the kitchen doorway—once there, she pushed the door hard against the rush of air. She leaned in with her shoulders, until the latch clicked, shutting the storm outside.

CHAPTER FOUR:
The Photograph

In the kitchen, Bibi paused, her insides shimmying with her fast-beating heart. *Breathe.* Her reflection in a mirror on the other wall showed her hair like an explosion. She smoothed it down.

She couldn't believe it. Eek, chased by a swarm of bees into the forest! Now what?

Well, obviously, she was on her own. If she didn't go after Eek, no one would.

She gritted her teeth, lowering her chin against the book in her arms, considering the frightening, awful idea. Go after Eek? For six months, she'd stayed out of the forest. The trees seemed to go on forever.

Could she do it? Grandma Ivy's voice echoed in her head: *I'm calling to make sure you take your pill this morning, dear.* Ugh. Normally, she took one before going outside. It helped with the hylophobia. But it felt like filling her head with oatmeal. It made it hard to think, and it would make it hard to search.

Bibi set her jaw, as she had often seen her mom do. No pill today. It wouldn't be easy—but Eek's life might depend on Bibi thinking clearly. Today must be different.

She ran to the hall closet, grabbing her school backpack and dumping her book in. She checked her phone—two bars. She'd take that, too—though she didn't think it would help. Her friends had stopped texting her after the hylophobia started. What had Grandma Ivy said? *That means they weren't really your friends, my dear.*

Bibi threw on her denim jacket and sneakers and paused. She had one more thing to get.

She sprinted to her parents' study, farther down the hall. Lonelier than the rest of the house, the room teemed with books abandoned in piles across the floor. Almost lost in the sound of the wind, a grandfather clock made a *tok, tok, tok* in one corner, like the trees in her nightmare. With a rabble of butterflies fluttering in her stomach, Bibi rifled through the paraphernalia on a desk—an astrolabe, a Zulu-to-English dictionary, her dad's telescope, her mom's almanac.

Hidden under a stack of handwritten letters, she found it: her favorite photograph of her parents, Nan Blundermuss and Bjorn Skovgaard, in a silver frame. She put it there six months ago—out of sight, to lessen the pain of missing them.

Bibi's eyes filled with tears. In the photo, Nan wore a gray cloak and a pair of Wellingtons. Long black braids framed her beautiful dark face, and she held a tree branch in front of her like a dagger—Bibi did not know why. Bjorn wore tinted goggles perched on top of his head, an axe holstered to his side, and a lab coat as pale as his skin. He smiled beneath a jet-black mustache and a day's worth of stubble.

They looked like two daredevils, on the verge of an adventure. Where had they gone? Why? Sometimes Bibi wondered if their disappearance was her fault. *Sometimes we have to accept things we can't understand,* Grandma Ivy had said. No. Bibi clutched her middle as the butterflies in her stomach changed to crows, pecking with a familiar pang.

"Come back," Bibi said, staring at the photo. "So I won't be scared of the trees."

The photo would help her in the forest. She took it out of its frame. Before she put it in her pocket, she noticed something she hadn't before. On the back—her mom's forceful handwriting. Hastily scribbled, like a to-do list. *Destroy Praetor Wight,* it said. *Prevent more wights. Find Anaspiritus.*

What? What could that mean? Bibi furrowed her brow.

Weeeeoooo! the wind said.

No time to wonder. Throat aching with the honey scent, Bibi jammed the photo into her jeans pocket, and ran back to the kitchen, until she stood once more in front of Eek's side door.

The bee buzz, though distant, resounded through the house, vibrating in Bibi's body. But the hard, heavy wind roared loudest of all—it felt like someone jabbing a bony finger at her temples. In the six months since her parents disappeared, she hadn't been in the forest once. Today she had no choice. She didn't know if they were gone for good, but she couldn't lose her cat, too.

Bibi took a deep breath, bracing. She threw open the door. Sound and scent and air came at her in a rush.

"Hold on, Eek!" she shouted, charging across the yard and into the forest.

CHAPTER FIVE:
Concentrate on Something Else

By the time Bibi made it past the first trees, the wind tapered off again—though the honey scent still hung thick in the air, accompanied by the heavy buzzing. Heart ramming against her ribs, she balled her hands into fists. But she did not vomit. She did not become dizzy or have a seizure. The hylophobia could overtake her at any moment, she knew, but if she moved quickly . . . maybe . . .

"Eek! Where are you?"

You won't believe what she's *scared of.* Well, she would show Ellery Finley and the other kids—she could do this. A few seconds in, the first drops of rain began to trickle down, like tiny seed pods, hitting the trees with a high-pitched patter. A surge of lightning stabbed the air, showing the tree branches chafing against each other, like jousting lances.

Sometimes prompted by the mere sight of a tree . . . so don't look! Ignore the trees. Concentrate on something else. Bibi stared at her old canvas sneakers as she moved, and as the rain drummed the back of her head.

She thought of the photograph in her pocket. Her mom's brown skin that always smelled nice, even at the end of the day. Her mom calling her *Acorn*. Her mom and Grandma Ivy and Bibi sharing the same last name, for reasons Bibi never understood. Her dad's laughter, like the low notes on a pipe organ. His skin pale as a ghost. Their family trip to the Oregon coast a few years ago—they had hiked a beach forest, and Bibi had climbed the trees.

. . . *the trees*—no! Ignore the trees. Concentrate on something else.

She went on. The sweetness in her nostrils nauseated her— the air swirling like a sea of honey. *BUZZ.* What else could she concentrate on? What about . . . *sawubona.* Her mom had taught her that word. A Zulu word. Her mom didn't know Zulu, but her ancestors came from South Africa. *Sawubona* meant "good day." Grandma Ivy once made a beautiful painting of a South African tree called a baobab.

. . . *a tree called a baobab*—no! Ignore the trees. Concentrate on something else.

The buzz made Bibi's teeth and bones shake as she walked, like being in the school bus when it bumped over the old dirt road. School . . . maybe think of something from school? Name all the presidents, in order. Something she learned two years ago, in fifth grade. Who knows why? Washington, Adams, Jefferson,

Madison . . . Harrison, Tyler, Polk. Fillmore? No! Taylor, then Fillmore. Taylor, Fillmore . . . Lincoln.

Lincoln? Yes, Lincoln.

Lincoln in a log cabin.

A log cabin made from . . .

"UGH!" Bibi hugged her abdomen. It always came back to trees. *Inhale. Exhale.* "Eek! Where *are* you?"

Concentrating on something else didn't work—didn't stop the hylophobia. Her gut began to clench, and she choked back a dry heave—as if her body wanted to turn itself inside-out. *BUZZ.*

So wet—the rain soaked through her clothes and backpack. She feared her photo and phone would be ruined. So far into the forest—would she ever find her way out? She groaned. Eek might be just ahead, behind the next stump or standing snag. She couldn't give up. She tried to signal her cat with a whistle. But her mouth tasted papery, and only a pathetic *hiss* came out—too soft under the loud *BUZZ.* She choked up another dry heave and paused to double over.

Why hadn't she taken a pill? Why why why! She felt a flu-ish chill. The hylophobia came at her hard—like a bully pummeling her abdomen. "You're afraid!" each blow said. "You're afraid!" Like the kids whispering at school.

BUZZ. If only her parents would come back. If only . . .

She had never been so nauseous. It seemed someone squeezed her stomach—trying to wring it out like a wet rag. Could hylophobia kill her? Maybe. Maybe that would be better than this. *No, don't think that!* Her breath sharpened, shortened. She put her hands to her knees.

20

And just when the bee buzz grated to a fever pitch, it stopped, as if turned off by a switch—leaving only the sound of the rain, its millions of drops striking the leaves in a delicate, pinging symphony.

Sicker than ever, Bibi peered out at the forest. Why had the buzz stopped? The honey scent remained strong.

She paused.

Something small and black, a stone's throw away, stared curiously at a sapling.

Her cat.

CHAPTER SIX:
Reunion

"*Sawubona*, Eek!" Bibi cried.

Eek snapped her head around in surprise.

"*Mrow! Sawubona*, Bibi!" She darted over, tail straight as a flagpole. Bibi fell to her knees on the forest floor's cold ooze, weak with relief, running a still-shaking hand across Eek's wet fur. Her body ached from nausea, but the simple, obvious love in Eek's green eyes made everything better.

"What are you doing here?" Eek said over the drone of the rain. "What about your hylophobia!"

Bibi nodded languidly. "I came to save you from the bees. Let's go home!"

At that, the buzz returned—low, quiet, close. Where were they? Bibi looked up, and small black flecks zipped down. A bee struck her cheek—harmlessly, but she flinched. More hit her shoulders and neck before flying on. Eek swiveled her head one way, and then the other—and the bees began swirling around them, like a little asteroid belt, buzzing louder.

Eek crept back, taking cover between Bibi's legs, tail lashing like mad, head cocked. Yet the bees did not sting.

"What do they want?" Bibi said.

"Beats me!" Eek whined a high meow. "But I don't think they'll sting us." So many bees gathered that they made a black blob, which moved to hover and burble near the sapling.

The sapling. Bibi stared. It was odd, somehow—out of place. She didn't recognize the tree type. It stood smaller than the others—twice her height, but below where the sun would reach on a clear day—with gray bark, and thin leaves. How had it gotten here?

The buzzing swarm got so loud that it drowned out the pelting rain—so loud that the sound stopped being a buzz and became almost a word.

"*Aaayyy*," the bees said.

Huh? Bibi did a double take and came close to laughing. Could she trust her own ears? A bee *voice?* But not the voice of the bees. A familiar voice—like someone she loved, through a bad phone connection, distorted and distant. She shivered in her wet clothes and wiped the rain from her glasses.

"*Aaayyyccc*," the bees said, molding the sound, making it more recognizable. Almost human. "*Aaayyyccccooorrr*."

Almost human? That voice!

"*Aaayyycorn*. Acorn!"

"*MOM?*"

CHAPTER SEVEN:
Nan Blundermuss Gets a Message Through

Bibi and Eek exchanged shocked glances. Eek's green eyes seemed as if they might pop out of her head, and her teeth chattered incomprehensibly in the downpour.

"I wish I could explain," the voice of Nan Blundermuss buzzed on, through the bees. "But I don't have time."

"M-Mom?" Bibi said, standing so she could take a step toward the swarm. Despite her fear, she fumbled at the air in front of her, wondering if her mom had become invisible. "Where are you?"

"Soon, we'll be together again," buzzed the voice.

The bee cloud rippled, and then hovered still again. Bibi's stomach kept twisting painfully, but excitement began bubbling like a fountain inside her, too. She stood on tiptoes, trying to look over and around the bees. Maybe her mom was behind them?

"Mom!" Bibi said again. "Where are you?"

"This will not make sense at first," the voice said. "But our lives depend on *you*."

Bibi's heart thumped in her ears. Our *lives*? "Mom, where *are* you? And where is Dad?" She thought of the photo and the strange words on the back. "What is Praetor Wight? And Anaspiritus? And why—"

The bees interrupted her, buzzing faster.

"Climb the Ash sapling in front of you."

Bibi staggered back a few steps, ignoring the rain beading on her glasses. The *sapling!*

"Mom!" she yelled, frustration tearing at her voice. She flapped her arms over her head, as if signaling someone far away. "Mom, are you there?"

"I don't think she can hear you!" Eek said, looking up from the forest floor as the bee cloud roiled. "I think the bees are repeating something she said!"

Bibi clasped her head in her hands. That couldn't be right. This must be a trick. "Where *is* she?"

In a *whoosh*, Eek scurried up the trunk of the Ash sapling, and onto the lowest branch, a little higher than Bibi's head. "*Mrow!*" she said, pinning her ears back. "Let's find out! Your mom said to climb. You can do it, Bibi—climb!"

Bibi's face flushed. She shook her head and backed away. She imagined the sapling's branches wrapping around her— squeezing the life out of her.

"What? I can't, Eek! Come down! Grandma Ivy will be worried. We've got to go home!"

Eek's tail hung over the edge of the branch, curling slightly at the tip. The fur along her back cowlicked in the rain.

"Your mom said to *climb*," Eek said. "Don't you see? Maybe that's so we can find out what happened to your parents! You're in the forest already—it can't get worse!"

Bibi closed her eyes. Her arms and legs jerked uncontrollably, as if threatening to leave her body. It *could* get worse! She knew it. Climbing the tree would mean touching the tree. That would be horrible! Her stomach wrenched. She would throw up. She might never stop!

She clamped her lips tight, as the cold raindrops struck her face like pin-pricks. The bee voice took on an angry edge.

"Acorn," it buzzed. "I wish I could explain, but I don't have time."

"You just said that!" Bibi opened her eyes, stomping her foot on the forest floor, splashing mud at the base of the sapling. She pointed to the bees. "What did you do to my mom?"

Eek stood on the branch, blinking and trying to shake the water from her coat. "I think the bees are our friends, Bibi!" she said, whipping her tail.

"Soon, we'll be together again," the bee voice went on.

"No!" Bibi said, covering her ears. "Stop it, stop it, stop it!"

The bees hovered in their inky cloud, as the rain came down in heavier and heavier sheets. "Climb the Ash sapling in front of you."

Bibi gritted her teeth. This couldn't be happening. Maybe she never woke up this morning—maybe the nightmare hadn't ended. Why would her mom want her to climb this sapling?

She fought the feeling of falling into a hole that kept getting deeper and deeper.

She wanted to grab Eek out of the sapling. Instead, without warning, the sapling *wriggled*—all by itself, like a wet dog, spraying Bibi with more rain. Eek almost fell—catching herself just in time, hissing and clinging to the branch.

The shaking stopped.

An ominous flurry of leaves littered down. Briefly, Bibi forgot her fear. She stared, her mouth agape.

"Did that sapling *move?*" she said.

Before Eek could answer, the sapling made a splitting, cracking sound. With the cat still in it, it grew taller, doubling its size in a few seconds. And then it stopped again.

Looking up at Eek—much higher now—Bibi unthinkingly reached for one of the sapling's lowest branches, holding firm—as if to prevent the young tree from growing more. At that, the bees buzzed louder.

"Eek . . ." Bibi said, keeping still and speaking through clenched teeth. "Please . . . get . . . *down!*"

Too terrified to move, Eek dug her claws deeper into the wood. The sapling's crown bobbed in the rain and wind.

"*Eek!*" Bibi's shock faded, replaced by a rush of fear. "Get out of the tree—*now!*"

As she grasped the branch, green spots faded in and out before her eyes. She was touching the tree . . . touching the tree touching the tree touching the tree. She saw her skin against the bark and fought the nausea of her hylophobia. She thought of the book in her backpack.

The sapling gave another, much harder shake, with another splitting, cracking sound. And this time, when it grew, it did not stop—yanking her up violently.

CHAPTER EIGHT:
The Tree-Rocket

The air blew cold on Bibi's wet skin as the sapling erupted upward. She forced herself to hold on—she couldn't lose Eek again! She wrapped her legs around the trunk. The forest zoomed by, as if the earth was sucking the other trees down.

But the earth was not sucking the other trees down. The sapling was growing, like a rocket shot—ten feet, twenty, thirty—climbing higher and higher toward the forest canopy.

Eek caterwauled. They couldn't jump off—they were too high, rising so fast that Bibi felt like her insides were back on the ground. The Ash sapling shoved up alongside trees that had towered overhead a moment ago, and toward the dark rainclouds. Twigs and leaves scratched at Bibi's face, and birds and squirrels scrambled out of the way, with little terrified cries.

"Mom!" Bibi clung like a climber stranded on a steep cliff. Eek hissed at the rain, as the bees flew skyward to join them.

"Soon, we'll be together again!" the bees buzzed, in the voice of Nan Blundermuss—trailing them higher, as the Ash tree rose.

Growing thicker and taller, the Ash tree burst through the understory, like a stone through a skylight. It soared above the forest canopy, with the emergent trees, hundreds of feet above the ground. Still it grew, at a breakneck pace, carrying Bibi and Eek upward into the drenching rain.

Quickly, fog surrounded the tree, harsh and wet on Bibi's cheek. They could no longer see the forest, or the part of the trunk below them. Her arms coated in frost, Bibi breathed in faint white puffs, and a sharp wind bit her ears and nose.

"Eek," she stammered. "I think we're in the clouds!"

"I kn-kn-know!" Eek answered, her little teeth clicking together.

Through pulses of dancing lightning, the tree-rocket ascended out of the carpet of white-gray, above the clouds and into the brilliant blue sky, under a glaring sun that threatened to sear Bibi's eyes. The bees still trailed them.

The wind overpowered all other sounds, pressing like a cold blade against Bibi's skin. It hurt to breathe. It hurt to hold on. Numb fingers, toes, arms, legs . . . icy veins . . .

The blue sky turned gray and the gray turned black.

CHAPTER NINE:
Across the Cosmos

The tree kept going, through vast, quiet darkness—somewhere new. Damp lingered on Bibi's clothes and hair, and Eek's fur. But the frost disappeared. The stabbing cold and the sound of the wind disappeared.

Eek took her paws from her eyes. "Look!" she said, her squeaky voice floating into the deep silence.

Bibi's head ached as she tried to take in the scene. Below them, Earth—a ball of blue and green and white, with the tree growing from it. The planet got farther away with each breath. She reached toward it, helplessly. "Come back," she whispered.

"*Mrow*—we're in space!" Eek said. *The Cosmos*—Bibi's dad's favorite word for it. Once, long ago, he taught her how to use a telescope. *See how the night sky goes on forever, Beebs?*

She checked her pocket. The photo of her parents—still there, damp but not ruined.

The bees clustered together higher on the trunk, forming a bulbous black lump. Their buzzing dwindled to a hum, until they spoke again, in what seemed to be their own voice—more monotonous than before.

"We are sorry to have frightened you, Bibi Blundermuss. We did not know how to get you into the forest—so we chased your cat there."

Bibi turned to Eek, then back to the bees. "Where are you taking us?" she said. But the hum stopped, and instead of answering, the insects went to sleep.

Bibi's eyes adjusted, and stars flickered on in the distance, one by one, like tiny signal lamps. Their cold, dim light showed the massiveness of the tree—its leaves blanket-size, the branch beneath her broad enough to lie down on.

Riding through space on a giant tree. A giant *tree*! Wobbly with the realization, Bibi lay down on the surface of the branch—clutching her middle as the hylophobia gnawed at her, like a wolf worrying a bone. Eek, purring, tried to comfort her with a head butt.

Long inhale. Long exhale. "At least we don't have astrophobia, Eek," Bibi mumbled. "That's the fear of outer space."

Eek gave a drawn-out growl, tinged with regret. "But how can we *be* in outer space?" she said. In the infinite dark, an aura of red-orange rose from the tree, covering them. Bibi had just enough strength to point. "Maybe that's a force field, protecting us?"

Eek shrugged. Her tail curled and uncurled, as if with a mind of its own. And the tree grew and grew.

Time passed, as they traveled through the Cosmos on the growing Ash tree. Bibi gazed at the passing stars. Could her mom really be out here somewhere? Overwhelmed by nausea, she stayed on her side on the giant branch, squeezing the straps of her backpack, wishing she could throw up and get it over with. She just wanted to be back in the house, with Eek and Grandma Ivy.

Later, a light appeared above them. Bibi found the strength to stand, queasily. The light came from the golden rays of a star—much closer than the others, moving at them with alarming speed, warming them with its heat.

"Eek," Bibi whispered, keeping her eyes on the star, but jostling her napping cat. When Eek saw the star, she stood too, hissing, fur on end.

Refracted by some contour of space, the star moved to one side. A small planet—hued like the earth, but more vibrant—came toward them next, like a blue-green ball hurled by a giant.

"Is that where we're going?" Eek asked, her voice on edge, as she paced along the branch like a nervous kitten.

Bibi didn't know. Her stomach, already twisted by hylophobia, began turning somersaults at the thought of passing into a new world. And they moved out of the black Cosmos, and into the light of the blue-green planet.

CHAPTER TEN:
Upside-Down

The loud, harsh scream of another cold wind assaulted them as they entered another blue sky. Bibi's eyes watered madly behind her glasses. Eek, yowling again, flattened her body against the branch, digging deeper with her claws.

"I'm sorry, Bibi!" she said. "We should have stayed on the ground back in the forest!"

"Just hold on!" Bibi called back, as the cold air hammered them from all sides. Gravity let go of them from beneath, pulling them from above. Above became below: topsy-turvy, they dove toward the ground, held in the tree by the speed of its plunge.

Bibi's backpack slipped, and *An Encyclopedia of Fear* tumbled out. Vandal-like, the wind threw it against a higher branch, whipping it open, and tearing out page after page, until the binding cartwheeled away into the nothingness of sky.

"No!"

Straining against the merciless wind, Bibi zipped her backpack closed and forced herself to lay with Eek on the branch, using all her strength to wrap her arms and legs around it, feeling the ridged bark pressing against her abdomen like the knuckles of a bony fist. Below, a valley surrounded by black mountains rushed up to meet them, as the tree-rocket dove.

"We're going to crash, Bibi!" Eek yelled. "*Mrow!*"

Closer and closer came the valley between the mountains. And in the valley—a forest. The worst possible place to plummet into—a sea of strange trees. Even from this distance, Bibi saw their branches reaching up—black, spiky, long and leafless. With her heart jammed in her throat, she screwed her eyes shut.

"*NO!*"

At last, with a prolonged, ear-splitting *crack*, the tree slowed, and slowed, and slowed. Bibi worried she might throw up everything she had ever eaten, as all the blood rushed to her head. But the tree kept slowing, stubbornly, until it stopped.

It hung still in the air.

Bibi opened her eyes, hanging upside-down, as several giant Ash tree leaves littered the sky around her, like huge green parachutes. Her arms and legs began to shake, and she started slipping. She and Eek climbed to the top side of the branch.

Then, unexpectedly, the tree gave one last jolt—and this time Eek lost her footing and slipped off.

"*Eek!*"

Meowing loudly, Eek tumbled from the upside-down tree into the black forest. Alarmed, the bees broke off from where they clumped against the Ash trunk, buzzing down after the cat. From branch to branch, Eek ricocheted, as the bee cloud followed her, lower and lower. In seconds, both vanished into the darkness below, like stones dropped into a bottomless well.

Everything quieted, except for Bibi's rapid-fire panting. She clutched her head, trying to still her clamoring thoughts—trying not to hyperventilate.

"Cats have nine lives," she said. "Cats know how to fall. Cats *always come back!*" She swiped away tears. She cupped her hands and shouted into the murk below. "I will *not* lose you again, Eek! I'm coming!"

Hands trembling, she climbed down to the crown of the Ash tree, so that she dangled just above the top of the black forest. Fighting her fear, she lowered a leg until her foot touched one of the spiky branches. There. It felt hard and unyielding, like stone. She thought of a trip her class took last year, to the American Museum of Natural History, in New York City. There had been a petrified tree on display. Were these trees petrified, too?

Bibi swung her other leg down. Sensing that the spiky branch could support her, she let go of the Ash branch. Before she knew what she had done, it sprang back, out of reach.

She glared up at the Ash tree—still in the sky above her, too high to touch. "*Stay,*" she ordered.

But the Ash tree trembled, shedding more leaves. It groaned—and began rising, slowly at first, retreating back into the blue sky. Back the way they had come—like a fishing line being reeled in.

"Wait!" Bibi said, extending a hand up after the tree as it sped its ascent. "Come back!"

It did not listen. Higher and higher it went, past the layers of blue and the distant clouds, making Bibi feel ever smaller—so small she might disappear. She shielded her eyes from the bright sun, desperate not to lose sight of her only way home. But in a breath or two, she did.

The tree had left her alone, stranded at the other end of the Cosmos, staring into the cold sky.

Inhale. Exhale. Dread. Terror. Anguish. Bibi tried to smother each emotion as it hit her. She tried not to cry. She tried not to think about anything. She steadied herself on the hard, black branch, looking down with wet eyes, and calling into the impenetrable gloom of the alien forest once more.

"Eek!" she said, her voice cracking. No sound or light came from below. No cat. No bees. Nothing.

Though Bibi had never been so scared, she set her jaw. "I am going to find my cat, and my mom and dad, and get out of this place," she said. And she began to climb down into the black forest, branch by terrible branch.

CHAPTER ELEVEN:
The Tree Graveyard

Though Bibi hadn't climbed a tree in six months, she hadn't forgotten how. Desperate to get out of this one, she didn't take long to reach the ground.

"Eek!" she said, stepping onto the forest floor. "Mom?" No one answered. No bees, no book. Everything from home had been swallowed by the nothingness of the alien forest.

Bibi's stomach cramped. She hugged her backpack tighter and rubbed her temples. She checked her phone. Searching . . . searching . . . battery almost dead. She put it away. What was this place? The trees' dark branches jutted at odd angles, as if angrily drawn with black Sharpee. Tucked around them and overhead, a curtain of white mist blotted out the sun and sky. An odor of sour soil rose from the ground.

Bibi thought again of the petrified tree in the museum, and

she knew—these trees were dead. "This isn't a forest," she said. "This is a graveyard." Her small voice evaporated into the mist.

A tree graveyard.

"Eek!" she said again, as the hylophobia rumbled worse in her stomach, and then began constricting around it like a python. She swatted at the air, trying to push the fear away. *Stop it, stop it, stop it!* Don't look at the trees!

But they were everywhere. If Ellery Finley could see her now. No—he'd never believe it. Not only a forest—a *dead* forest, on another world. Bibi wanted her book. She wanted her cat. She wanted her parents—they'd make the fear go away. The journey had sapped her strength. Her mind raced with memories of the trees in her nightmare. The clawlike branches. The *tok, tok, tok.*

She looked at the real trees. The jagged, petrified branches, like the charred bones of alien giants. *No.*

Her hands wouldn't stop shaking. Clouds crept into the edges of her vision. What had her book said? *Hylophobia progresses through a range of symptoms—beginning in nausea, and moving to dizziness, seizures, and ultimately a comatose state.*

So far, she had only been nauseous. But now dizziness began. She teetered—like on the Tilt-a-Whirl she had ridden during the Oregon Coast trip. There, the other kids had laughed at her when her knees buckled. Here, the trees tilted around her—they seemed to be laughing, too.

About to fall over, she stopped when a rustling sound caught her ear. A timid, high-pitched voice said, "Welcome to Falanthrow Forest—do you need help?"

Bibi snapped alert, shaking her head, trying to clear it.

The trees kept tilting—but breathing hard, she managed to turn toward the voice.

A four-legged animal emerged from the mist.

She recognized it instantly. Elk—a kind of deer. Also known as wapiti. She had learned that from the American Museum of Natural History, too. She had seen a diorama there, with four elk in it.

This elk was very scared, and very young—about her size, with rake-thin legs, a torso that showed his ribs, and an unkempt tuft of dark-brown hair between his ears, where antlers should have been. A white rump contrasted with his clay-colored, mottled coat. His nose twitched furiously.

Barely able to control her surprise, Bibi worried she might scare him off—he looked as if he might fall apart if she so much as breathed on him. And yet—hadn't he asked if she needed help? She spoke slowly through her dizziness, her trembling voice a hush:

"Yes—can you help me?"

The elk opened his mouth to answer, but then whipped his head to one side, as if he had seen something in the mist—something that scared him more than she did. He waited, perfectly still. Bibi struggled to steady herself, seeing nothing.

After a moment, the elk made a furtive noise. "We must go!" he whispered, turning back to her. "Get on!"

Go? Go where? Why? "I can't!" she said. She had to find Eek. Her head spun, and her stomach flip-flopped—the hylophobia worsening.

And then she saw what he had seen.

A few hundred feet away, long shadows glided through the mist.

"Ghosts?" she whispered.

Not ghosts. Cats! And not just any cats—enormous white lions. Bigger than any she had seen back on Earth—almost as big as cars. Their pale sleek fur blended with the mist, making them seem to float—majestic and silent.

Bibi counted. One, two, three of them. Two lions and a lioness. They were upwind, moving perpendicular to her. They were far enough away that they hadn't noticed her—but for how long? Their brows were furrowed and intent, and soon, their peculiar scent—a mix of blood, iron, urine, and bile—joined with the sour soil smell, and the air became repulsive.

The little elk whispered, lips hardly moving. "Trolliclawians. We have to go. Please get on."

But Bibi, thinking of Eek, remained still—so still that it hurt. She held her breath. That saved her from the awful smell—until she needed air again.

Nausea. Dizziness. A dead forest. A terrified elk. Lions called Trolliclawians. What next?

As if in answer, one of the lions stopped abruptly, turned in her direction, and said, in a voice that seemed to sizzle like forest fire, "Who's there?"

CHAPTER TWELVE:
Valmyr

In front of Bibi, the little elk squirmed behind the closest tree, as if trying to find a way to climb into the folds of its bark.

The lion who had stopped bared his dagger-like teeth—Bibi saw them stained red. He had not seen her yet, but a deep snort told her he had picked up her scent, or maybe the little elk's. Her throat cinched with panic.

The red-toothed lion's comrades paused, following his gaze. He swiveled his head, like a gun turret seeking its target. If he were to move his eyes a little more to the left . . .

"Is it woodskulls, Lord Valmyr?" said the lioness. Bibi saw flecks of gold in her white coat.

Valmyr, the red-toothed lion, did not answer. He glowered, sniffing deeper and scanning the dead forest, harsh yellow eyes like searchlights in the mist. Bibi tried to make herself look tree-like—to blend with the forest. *No! Don't think of the trees.* She couldn't let the hylophobia get worse—not now. One fear at a time.

"Lord Valmyr!" said the third Trolliclawian, drawing the red-toothed lion's attention back. "Look!"

Valmyr pulled a face. "Must I be everywhere at once?" he said, turning from the direction of Bibi and the little elk, toward a new thing—a freckled cloud that spiraled lazily around one of the dead trees, directly in the Trolliclawians' path. Then Bibi heard it: buzzing in the mist.

The bees!

They wobbled in the air, as if disoriented. Why? Bibi remembered beekeepers at one of the farms near her house using smoke to slow their bees down. Maybe the mist had the same effect on these bees?

As the lions watched, one by one the bee swarm landed on the tree trunk, creating an inky girdle around it. When the last of the bees landed, their buzz dwindled into silence.

A look of disgust spread like a stain across Valmyr's face. He stepped over to the bee tree. The bees did not move. The mist seemed to have made them dormant.

"Gorka, these are bees. Pests."

Without ceremony, Valmyr raised a paw, wide as the head of a shovel. Bibi bit her lip—and he swung, flattening a clump of the bees against the tree trunk with a single sickening *thwap*.

Bibi gasped and touched the little elk's hide in horror.

"Climb on my back," he whispered, though his legs were

shaking like reeds in a choppy wind. "We must flee, while the lions are distracted."

Bibi pulled her hand away and shook her head. She desperately *wanted* to leave—but she had to find Eek first. And the bees—they knew where her mom was! No—she couldn't leave. She had to help somehow.

Some of the bees who had been spared Valmyr's first blow bravely tried to fly at him. But they could not handle the mist. Once in the air, they meandered like dying moths to the forest floor, becoming lost in the debris of dead leaves and dirt. Valmyr, still shaking smooshed insects from his paw, raised it again to take another swing. But before he could, a high-pitched voice cried out: "Leave them alone!"

Another shape appeared next to the red-toothed white lion, much smaller in comparison. Pure black against the white mist. Green eyes. A tail that stuck up like a flagpole.

Gooseflesh shot up Bibi's arms.

The black shape was Eek—hissing at Valmyr, her hackles raised.

CHAPTER THIRTEEN:
Flight

Bibi covered her mouth to keep from shouting. Did Eek think she could stop this lion? Had she lost her mind?

But to Bibi's surprise, Valmyr's piercing gaze eased at the sight of the little black cat. He paused—then sat back on his haunches and broke into a fusillade of laughter. The other lions smiled with chagrin.

"Brave black catling!" Valmyr said. "You're feisty. You'll make a good warrior one day—when you are grown and get your white coat." Smile fading, he narrowed his eyes and looked at the others. "Of course, since she *isn't* grown, and she *hasn't* gotten her white coat, she has no business being on this patrol. Gorka and Alenka—which of you brought her along?"

Alenka—the lioness with flecks of gold in her white coat—started. She turned to Gorka—the lion who had found the bees—and then back to Valmyr. "Neither of us, my lord," she said. "We've never seen this catling." Gorka frowned, as if to say, *It wasn't me.*

Valmyr flashed his red teeth. Eek sank to her abdomen in the leaves, and Bibi balled her hands into fists. Even from this distance, she could see the tremors shaking her cat's body. *Eek Eek Eek!*

Valmyr sniffed in Alenka's direction. "Very well. Deal with her."

Alenka nodded. She swooped over to Eek and took the little black cat in her mouth. Bibi couldn't help herself. "*NO!*" she screamed.

By the time she realized that Alenka had no intention of *eating* Eek—but had merely picked her up by the scruff of her neck, as if she were a kitten—it was too late. The Trolliclawians had turned toward Bibi and the little elk. This time, they had no doubt that someone was there.

"Woodskulls!" Valmyr called furiously into the mist, voice like a scythe cutting through the understory. "Show yourselves— you know you can't escape!" Alenka and Gorka scowled into the forest, looking for the source of the scream.

"*Get on, get on, get on!*" the little elk said to Bibi, sucking air as if trying not to drown.

That's when Valmyr finally saw them. He seemed confused by Bibi for a fleeting second. He'd probably never seen a creature like her before. Shaking off his surprise, he lowered his head and charged. The others followed in his wake—Alenka still carrying Eek, Gorka roaring with rage.

At the sight of the lions speeding at her like torpedoes, Bibi scrambled onto the young elk without thinking, belly-down, wrapping her arms around his neck. "Go, go, go!"

He needed no urging, and turned and fled, hooves tearing at the ground, tuft of dark-brown hair bobbing. Bibi barely held on. *Eek Eek Eek*, she thought, as the mist and the dead trees blew past.

She felt the elk's muscles toiling. She heard the lions' roars sounding behind them, like the rumble of a forest fire, flames getting closer, singeing her heels. The elk leapt and dodged and scurried between the dead trees. How foolish to think they could get away! The lions were bigger and faster.

Bibi choked back a sob of terror. Would everything end here? Had she come all this way—fighting hylophobia, crossing the Cosmos—only to lose her cat, and miss her chance to find her mom, and maybe her dad? Killed by a red-toothed white lion in a dead forest? She was only twelve—her life hadn't even begun yet!

She closed her eyes and tried to shut everything out.

I'm sorry, Eek! I'm sorry, Grandma Ivy! I'm sorry, Mom and Dad!

CHAPTER FOURTEEN:
Living Trees

The little elk kept running.

Any second now . . . Bibi shut her eyes tighter, sure of the coming bloodshed.

She knew the lions were right behind them—she could hear their snarling breath, and the *pata-thump* of their paws. She could smell their blood-iron-urine-bile stink. She swore she could feel their wickedness coming down on her like a net. But still the little elk kept running—free, safe.

Afraid to open her eyes, Bibi wondered what was going on. What was taking so long? She counted ten . . . twenty . . . thirty seconds. *Pata-thump, pata-thump*, the lions' paws continued— but softer, as if they were falling behind. A trick? She opened her eyes a crack, turning to see.

She couldn't believe it.

The lions were still there, still led by Valmyr, but much farther behind. They hadn't been outrun—something else had slowed them. Even at a distance, and even as the little elk kept running, Bibi could see Valmyr's yellow eyes seething with rage. Why?

The light changed.

Bibi felt a burst of warmth on her skin, as if the little elk had jumped out of the chilly dark forest into the middle of a clear summer day. The light got so much brighter that she had to shield her face with her hand—almost losing her balance.

Onward the little elk ran. The roars faded behind them, sounding like cannons going off in the distance. Eyes adapting to the light, Bibi moved her hand away from her face and looked back. They were out of the mist—Bibi could see where it ended in a white wall. It got farther behind them with each stride.

And the lions? They had been left behind that wall somewhere. She couldn't see them at all anymore.

She and the little elk had escaped.

He stopped, chest heaving as he caught his breath. Bibi sat up and blinked—her eyes finally accustomed to the light, finally able to see where they were.

She stifled a gasp.

She and the little elk were still in the forest—but in this part, the sun shone, no longer hidden by the mist. The trees were not the scrawny, stony, pitch-black dead things from the tree graveyard. These trees were alive. Thriving. Tall as full-grown oaks and covered with dewy green leaves.

And then there were the trees' flowers.

Red-orange and star-shaped. Big as pinwheels. Bibi blinked again as a cascade of glitter descended gently from them, like sunlight filtering through clear deep water. She looked down at her open hands. Quickly, the falling glitter coated her palms in shimmering motes of silver and gold.

Bibi sniffed. The glitter smelled of ginger. Like the tea Grandma Ivy used to make. And as it fell it made a sound— enchanted, fragile as an old memory. A mellifluous pinging, like . . . wind chimes? Yes. Bibi thought of the percussion cabinet in the school band room. At lunchtime, she loved to take out the row of dangling metal tubes and run a finger across.

Bibi had never seen a forest like this—so beautiful that it almost made her forget her hylophobia.

"What happened?" she asked, when she could finally speak.

The little elk, still panting, scanned the closest trees, and then turned his head so he could see her. "We—we lost them," he said with obvious relief. "Pollen from the Falanthrow trees is deadly to the Trolliclawians. Valmyr and the others can't follow us here."

Falanthrow trees, in Falanthrow Forest. Bibi shuddered, trying not to think of it. And the pollen? He must have meant the glitter pouring out of the red-orange flowers. Unlike any pollen Bibi had seen.

She slid off the little elk's back until she stood on the forest floor. *Falanthrow trees.* As soon as her feet hit the ground, a wave of nausea hit, almost knocking her down. She held her stomach, like an overfull bucket of water she didn't want to spill.

51

But . . . Eek. But . . . Mom. Her shoulders sagged. She had to stay here until she found them. In fact . . . she and the little elk had escaped the lions, but there was no way around it—she had to go back to the black trees. She *had* to. Eek was still there.

"My name's Corineus," the little elk said, a curious look in his eye. "What's yours?"

She watched him shake the glitter-pollen from the dark-brown tuft between his ears, making a brief silvery halo around his head. She hunched her shoulders. No, she couldn't leave Eek. She couldn't.

"I'm Bibi. Thanks for your help, but I have to go back."

She saw the little elk's mouth open in silent surprise. In a daze, she turned—and with wobbly legs began walking back through the sparkling waterfalls of flower-glitter, toward the mist and black trees.

CHAPTER FIFTEEN:
Nan Blundermuss's Daughter

"Wait—*wait!*" Corineus said. "What are you doing?"

Bibi did not answer as she moved quickly between the ginger-scented trees, trying not to get too close to any of them. She stared straight ahead. Resisting the hylophobia would take all her concentration. The nausea bubbled in her belly, like the boil of a nasty soup. The dizziness made her lurch from side to side drunkenly.

Corineus's hooves crunched through the leaves as he went after her. "Please, don't go back to the dead forest," he said, voice rising. "It's—it's not safe! Don't you remember the white lions?"

Bibi barely had the strength to roll her eyes. Did he actually think she could have forgotten the white lions?

Focus. Inhale, exhale. The hylophobia waited zombie-like, ready to lunge at her from behind the trees. *Think about something else.* She saw the wall of white mist, just ahead. *Think about Eek. Think about Mom.*

"Please!" Corineus said.

Bibi found it hard to conceal her irritation, made worse by her roiling stomach and her spinning head. "You don't have to follow me, you know! Shoo!"

Getting back to Eek would take all her effort. Don't think of the trees, don't think of the trees, don't think of the trees . . . The wall of mist hovered maybe fifty feet away. Bibi closed her eyes, shaking her head. She longed to shed her fear, like an old skin. Like . . .

The eucalyptus trees near school. They shed their skin, too—in rolling strips that looked like old parchment. No—don't think of the trees! *You won't believe what* she's *scared of.*

"The dead trees can't protect you!" Corineus said. "The blooming trees can!"

Stop it, stop it, stop it. Eek and Mom. Eek and Mom.

Corineus still followed her. His voice seemed to echo in her head: *The dead trees. The dead trees. The DEAD TREES . . .*

And then it happened. Bibi, very close to the wall of white mist, stepped in a rut and lost her balance—and nearly fell into one of the trees. And as she righted herself, the hylophobia hit her harder than before—harder than ever. As if she had banged her head on a too-low ceiling. She reeled, ears ringing. The fear moved down her body, violently squeezing her middle, making her nausea worse—like food poisoning so bad she had to double over.

No, no, no! Not again. The forest spun around her.

Her nightmares. Her lost book. Her grandma—probably worried sick about her at that exact moment, coming back from garden club to find her gone. Suddenly the forest felt both bigger and smaller than before. Bigger because she'd never get out—alive or dead, the trees went on forever. Smaller because the trees seemed to close in on her—like the trees in her nightmares.

Bibi collapsed, and began to cry, in deep, soul-shaking sobs.

"NO, NO, *NO!*" she said, slamming her fists on the forest floor. "I can't do this!"

She sobbed and sobbed, making a large damp spot in the dirt and dead leaves. Corineus stopped, watching her.

After a few minutes of crying, Bibi's eyes began to throb—she sat up, wiping them. She felt Corineus waiting for her to speak. She tried to find the right words. "I don't want to be here," she said. Should she tell him about her hylophobia? What would he think? She braced for his ridicule. "The trees . . ."

Corineus looked at her, and then at the living trees around them both—and then back at her. "Are you . . . *scared* of the trees?"

Bibi reddened, looking away. A cascade of glitter-pollen sparkled down, as if the trees were politely trying to change the subject.

"But your mother's power!" the little elk said.

What? In mid-sniffle, Bibi stiffened. Had she heard him right? She studied his face.

Corineus took a step back, timidly. "You—you *are* Nan Blundermuss's daughter, aren't you?"

For a moment, Bibi couldn't move. She stood and stumbled over to him, lightheaded and breathing heavily. He tried to back away—but before he could, she hugged him around the neck, with all her might. She couldn't help it. The first piece of good news she had gotten in six months.

"*Yes!*" she said. "Do you know her? Where is she? Can you take me? Did *you* send the bees?" Bibi just knew that her mom would help her get rid of the hylophobia for good. She pulled back to look Corineus in the eyes, thinking of the photo in her pocket. "Do *you* know Praetor Wight, or Anaspiritus?"

But before he could answer, a tsunami of nausea and dizziness hit her.

The hylophobia hadn't gone anywhere. Worsening, it made her feel like she had swallowed a bowling ball and fallen out of an airplane. The hylophobia didn't care if Corineus knew Nan Blundermuss. It didn't care whether the trees were alive or dead. It only cared that Bibi remained in the forest. She had been fighting her fear all day. She couldn't fight it anymore. She swayed in place, feeling a seizure coming.

A seizure! That was what the book had said. And after that, she'd be comatose. She didn't know what that meant, exactly, except that it was like being dead. You kept breathing, and your heart kept beating, but everything else sank into nothingness. That would be the end—it would mean the hylophobia had finally won. She'd be helpless.

Corineus, alarmed, ducked his head under Bibi's arm. She tried to look at him. She felt him close, but her eyes wouldn't focus, and so he seemed to be moving away—like at the wrong

56

end of a telescope. He nudged her, and she understood: he wanted her to get on his back again.

"Don't worry, Bibi Blundermuss!" he said, voice urgent even as it seemed to float away. "Come on! I'll take you where there are no trees—I'll tell you about your mom."

Too sick to speak, using her last bit of strength, Bibi climbed onto Corineus's back once more—barely holding on as he resumed his run through the glittery forest.

PART TWO
THE HARROWING

CHAPTER SIXTEEN:
The Clearing

"Bibi Blundermuss—look!" Corineus said.

Bibi, still on the little elk's back, blinked her eyes open, gazing sideways. She had been drifting, so close to being unconscious. But she had not had a seizure.

Relief engulfed her like a warm bath. No trees. They were in a wide clearing of long yellow-brown grass. Dry and brittle, it swished in the breeze. Corineus slowed, and Bibi sat up, steadying herself.

Time had passed—how much? She looked around, temples aching. The living trees were distant—half a mile away, at least, bordering the clearing in all directions, their cascades of glitter-pollen falling every few minutes or so, making a sparkling curtain in the sun. Bibi couldn't smell the ginger from here, and the sound of wind chimes was barely audible. Was she far enough away?

Yes! She wanted to shout when she realized it. She no longer felt sick. For the first time since leaving the house that morning, her stomach relaxed—she had almost forgotten what that felt like.

The clearing seemed roughly the size of a small town—one of those Oregon high-desert towns, with a main street that you could only reach from a single highway exit. As Bibi studied it, a dark cloud, low to the ground, appeared at the other end.

More elk! A small herd ran toward them, making a far-off drumming noise in the grass.

"Who is it?" Bibi said as she watched.

"My sister, Yega-Woo, and my friends," Corineus said. Without waiting for Bibi's reply, he cantered toward them, as she held tight.

It did not take long for all the elk to meet in the middle of the clearing. There were five in the herd—three bucks and two does. They were all at least a head taller than Corineus—though they did not seem much older than him. They arrayed in a line, suffusing the air with musk so strong it made Bibi's eyes water at first.

One of the does—sleek and streamlined, with eyes that glistened like black river rocks—stepped forward and nuzzled Corineus. "Oh, Cori," she said. "You had us scared to death. Where did you go?"

Corineus stooped before her. "I'm sorry, Yega-Woo," he said. "I was in the dead forest. It was an emergency. I didn't have time to tell anyone."

The other elk exchanged surprised glances. "In the dead forest, eh?" said the largest buck, in a voice that clanged like a locomotive bell. Though a youngster like the others, he had a scar on one side that gave him a mature look. Bibi thought he might be the leader. His antlers, like those of the other bucks, were short and stubby, and covered with fuzzy velvet.

"Yes, Genza," Corineus said, still looking down, and shaking his tuft of hair out of his eyes.

Genza inhaled exaggeratedly, as if preparing to berate the other—then let out a ringing laugh. "Good job, little Cori! Going where the white lions are? Not bad for someone who hasn't gotten his woodskull yet, eh? What happened?"

Bibi didn't think an elk could blush, but Corineus seemed to then.

"Yes—what happened, Runt?" said the next-largest buck, clipping his words impatiently as his brindle coat bristled. "Aren't you going to tell us what you *found?*"

After a pause, Bibi realized he was referring to her. Corineus looked back, with anxious eyes that seemed to say, *Let them see you.* Carefully, she slid from his back, until she stood in the long dry grass up to her knees. She felt the weight of the elk's stares.

"Genza, Yega-Woo, everyone," Corineus said, lowering his head again. "This is Bibi Blundermuss . . . the Arbor Guardian's daughter."

More surprise came to the elk's faces—as if Corineus's words carried a jolt of electricity. Softly, the little elk continued. "She came from the Sky Tree."

63

Bibi wrinkled her brow and adjusted her backpack. The *Arbor Guardian?* What was Corineus talking about? She had a discouraging thought—what if he had her mixed up with someone else? Maybe this "Arbor Guardian" was another person's mom? She felt the creeping ache of disappointment—like watching a longed-for letter being ruined in the rain, before she could even read it.

Then Corineus added, even softer than before, "And . . . I saw Valmyr."

This time, the elk jolted more violently. "The king of the lions—so close?" said the second doe, her russet hide gleaming in the morning sun.

"Did he find out about our clearing?" said the bristly brindle buck.

Corineus shrugged. Bibi quickly realized that the elk must have had run-ins with Valmyr and the Trolliclawians before. They must have ended badly. She glanced again at Genza's scar.

Genza took a deep breath. "Aruna, Zezo—relax. The blooming trees will keep the Trolliclawians out of our clearing." He turned to Bibi. "The Arbor Guardian's daughter, eh? Yes—I see the resemblance."

Bibi tried to smile—but remained confused. If he saw a resemblance, maybe her mom really was this "Arbor Guardian." But what did *that* mean? Bibi had never heard of an Arbor Guardian. She knew "arbor" meant tree—like in "Arbor Day." But there was nothing to connect her mom and trees.

Well, except maybe for the forest next to their house back in Oregon.

And the mysterious fast-growing sapling that brought Bibi and Eek across the Cosmos.

And, okay—maybe the fact that they had landed in yet *another* forest.

Still . . .

"The real question," Genza continued, "is what you are doing here—eh, Bibi Blundermuss?"

Before Bibi could answer, Yega-Woo blinked in the bright sunlight. "Well, that's obvious, Genza. She's here to help us find her mother."

CHAPTER SEVENTEEN:
Friends and Foes

Bibi started. Now they were getting somewhere! She waved her hand to get the elk's attention.

"Actually," she said, "can *you* help *me* find Mom? And Dad? Um, and my cat, too?"

At the mention of Eek, the elk went rigid, ears and white tails alert, as if someone had tossed a match into the dry grass. "I *knew* it," said Zezo, the brindle buck.

Bibi realized her mistake—too late. They thought all felines—whether white lions or little black cats—were the same, didn't they? They probably didn't even *have* house cats here. She rubbed her forehead, searching for the right words.

"No—you don't understand!" she said. "My cat isn't like the white lions! She's small and black. She would fit in my backpack. She stood up to Lord Valmyr! She's good!"

Zezo's nostrils flared. "Why should we believe that?"

"Yeah, why should we believe that?" said the third buck, speaking for the first time, his voice heavy as mud.

Bibi heard her heart beating in her ears. She didn't know what to say.

Genza shot daggers at Zezo and the third buck, and then turned to Bibi again. "I am sorry, daughter of Nan Blundermuss. Zezo and Baranji are skeptical because, some time ago, the Arbor Guardian went into the dead forest. She promised to drive the white lions away. But we haven't seen her since, and the white lions are still there." He paused. "Zezo and Baranji think she joined them."

Bibi couldn't believe it. *Joined* the white lions? *Mom?* Even though they had attacked Bibi, too? She looked at Corineus—but he seemed to be waiting for Yega-Woo to say something. Yega-Woo, in turn, glared at Zezo and Baranji.

In a low and measured voice, Aruna the russet doe said, "Zezo and Baranji forget that the Arbor Guardian *saved* us."

Zezo smirked, and then kicked at the dry grass. "Saved us for life in this prison? Where we're grazing the grass down, and the brook will freeze over, come winter? *Trapped* us, more like."

Bibi balled her hands into fists. She wanted to respond—she didn't understand everything the elk were saying, but she was sure her mom hadn't come all the way here just to hurt them. She wouldn't abandon them if she promised to help. Bibi knew it—she knew her own mom better than they did.

Didn't she?

Corineus spoke softly. "Zezo—don't you see? The Arbor

67

Guardian's daughter is here because the Quickening is finally coming. It's a sign."

Zezo made a face, as if Corineus had mentioned an embarrassing relative.

"The Quickening has been coming for a long time, hasn't it, Runt?" he said. He cocked his head toward the forest. "How long since the Arbor Guardian left? Four Black Moons ago? Five? And yet the Harrowing remains." He narrowed his eyes. "Face it—the Quickening isn't coming. It's a lie."

Genza laughed. "And why would the Arbor Guardian lie to us?"

"How should I know?" Zezo said. "But when the lions have finished killing all the other elk, they'll come for us. Maybe they're coming for us already—Valmyr has never been so close." His gaze grew steely as he settled it on Bibi. "No, I'm not waiting for help from the Arbor Guardian. She's betrayed us, I'm sure. Falanthrow Forest belongs to the elk. Someday soon we'll have to go to war with the Trolliclawians ourselves. The sooner we face that, the better."

Baranji looked at his stout legs and echoed the other sluggishly. "The better," he said.

Bibi felt like the ground had opened beneath her. Tears welled in her eyes. The Harrowing? The Quickening? What were they talking about? She wanted to scream with confusion. "I thought you were going to help me find Mom!" she said to the group.

Genza looked at Bibi. Then, slowly, he stepped over to the brindle buck, until their eyes were inches apart. He stood a little taller, his stubby velvet antlers a little more threatening. The clearing got very quiet, except for the breeze that blew through the dry grass, making it hiss like sharpening knives. Genza leaned forward enough to force the other to step back. Zezo did not resist, but he did not take his eyes from Genza.

Genza spoke in a low, firm voice. "Zezo and Baranji, you will make the Arbor Guardian's daughter welcome. She can stay until her mother comes back—or until we figure out what she's doing here."

Zezo rolled his eyes. But it was settled. Without waiting for more discussion, Genza charged out in front of the others, whirling around to face them, head silhouetted in the sun. He spoke as if nothing had happened—his voice regaining its locomotive-bell clang.

"Now—we've got things to do, friends. Let's check the edge of our clearing and see if we can spot Valmyr. Can't have him getting through, can we? Maybe Zezo's right, and we will have to go to war with the Trolliclawians soon. If so, remember what the elders used to say, about the time before the forest—antlers and hooves will beat the white lions, eh?"

"Antlers and hooves will beat the white lions!" Aruna said. "Huzzah, huzzah!"

Without waiting, Genza charged toward the circumference of trees. Zezo paused long enough to give Bibi a dirty look—but then he followed, with Baranji and Aruna. The four elk moved swiftly through the tall grass.

Yega-Woo waited a moment longer, smiling at Corineus. "Try not to go missing again—okay, little brother?" she said with a wink. Then she charged away, too.

CHAPTER EIGHTEEN:
High Hill

What to do?

A hill rose at the other end of the clearing, sere and brown, without a single tree. *High Hill,* Corineus called it—a bit higher than the forest. "Now that the Quickening is coming," he said, "we can wait there."

"Why?" Bibi asked as they headed toward it.

"When the Quickening happens, we'll know exactly where your mom is."

That sounded promising. Bibi still didn't understand what he meant by "the Quickening"—but she was glad they wouldn't have to go back to the forest yet. How long had she been away from the trees—an hour, maybe? Despite the tension with Zezo, she already felt much better—stomach calm, head clear. She wanted to stay that way as long as possible. But she wanted to keep searching for her mom and Eek, too.

The sun reached the middle of the sky as they walked through the parched grass. The light pressed like hot stones on the back of Bibi's neck. She was grateful for the lack of trees—but the lack of shade made her hot and hungry. She reached into her backpack, surprised and relieved to find a granola bar and a small bottle of water, left over from lunch a few weeks ago. She ate a little.

She felt lighter—as if the hylophobia had been a heavy chain she'd finally thrown off. Every once in a while, she caught a vague whiff of ginger. At the far end of the clearing, Genza and the others grazed just this side of the trees and glittering pollen, keeping an eye out for Valmyr and the white lions.

Bibi wanted more answers as she followed Corineus up High Hill.

"When did the Arbor . . ." she started to ask—then stopped herself. No. She didn't want to use that name. She cleared her throat. "When did *my mom* get here?" she said.

Corineus twitched his triangle of a white tail, vainly trying to keep away a flurry of gnats that had decided to follow him.

"Six Black Moons ago," he said. "She came out of the Sky Tree—like you." He scanned the incline, leading her along a switchback, his tuft of hair bobbing up and down with his steps. "Right after the Harrowing killed Falanthrow Forest."

That word again. "What *is* the Harrowing?" Bibi said.

Corineus's voice grew morose as they climbed, seeming

out of place in the increasing daylight. "The Harrowing is the white mist," he said.

"Well, why do you call it that? It sounds dangerous."

"It *is* dangerous. The Harrowing is a disease, Bibi Blundermuss. A tree sickness. It killed all the trees. That's how the white lions got in."

Bibi felt a flare of gooseflesh, despite the warmth. *Pollen from the Falanthrow trees is deadly to the Trolliclawians,* Corineus had said. *Valmyr and the others can't follow us here.* She lowered her voice as they kept climbing. "Got in?"

"Yes. They weren't always here. We weren't either. A long time ago, all of us lived in the Black Crest Mountains—the kingdom of the lions. There, elk were mercilessly hunted."

High Hill reached a little higher than the tallest Falanthrows, and as they neared the top, Bibi began to make out the mountains beyond. She shivered, remembering how ominous they had seemed when seen from the Ash Tree.

"Then we discovered that the Trolliclawians had a weakness: the Falanthrow trees," Corineus said. "All the trees were alive back then. If you went in the forest, you were safe. So Falanthrow Forest became our new home, and we thrived. Soon, there were almost as many elk as trees."

He spoke quickly, as if he had been holding onto his words for too long. The higher they got, the hotter it got. Bibi tried to imagine what Falanthrow Forest had looked like before the Harrowing—how the whole forest must have sparkled with pollen, like the ring of living trees currently protecting the clearing. Probably so bright that it blinded you.

"So, what happened then?"

Corineus stooped as he continued walking. "When the Harrowing came, the lions entered the forest, and began killing elk—elders first. Everyone scattered and fled, but the six of us friends stayed together. Maybe other elk survived—I don't know. Valmyr was the most violent of all. He was afraid of nothing—not the toughest bull, not the biggest antlers. Genza got that scar from him while trying to save his parents." He trailed off, catching his breath as the incline got steeper.

Valmyr. The name cut sharp as a butcher knife. The thought of those red teeth rattled Bibi. The elk seemed so young. If their parents were gone, that made them orphans. Thank goodness her own parents were only missing—not dead.

She shivered again. Her parents *were* only missing, right?

"This is it," Corineus said. "We'll be able to see the Quickening from here."

Bibi stopped to look around. They had reached the top of the hill—a rounded plateau about the size of a mini-mall parking lot. The raised view of the sparkling trees showed the ring they made around the clearing. Bibi began to understand. Everything within the sparkling tree ring was safe. Everything beyond it—mist-drenched blackness extending for what seemed like miles toward the mountains that loomed on all sides—was not.

But one thing still confused her.

"If the Harrowing killed the forest, why are the glittering trees still alive?" she said finally. "Why *those* trees?"

Corineus raised his brow, as if he didn't know how to

respond. "Bibi Blundermuss," he said, his voice almost a whisper. "Your mother did that. To protect us."

Bibi felt her mouth go dry. She couldn't have heard him correctly.

"What?"

He spoke slowly. "That's what an Arbor Guardian *is*—a witch who can heal dead trees."

Bibi took a step back. A witch? Who can heal dead trees? No. Impossible.

Seeing the disbelief on her face, Corineus bobbed his head vigorously. "It's true!"

No. Grandma Ivy would have known. Somebody would have said something! Maybe her mom had a secret, but that would be too big of a secret for anyone to keep.

"But—*how*?" Bibi said, trying to find the words. "How could she make the dead trees sprout leaves again and pour out the glittery pollen, keeping the lions away?" She couldn't imagine it.

Corineus shrugged. "She could, and she did. Your mother saved our lives, Bibi Blundermuss. No matter what Zezo or Baranji say."

But if her mom had healed the trees around the clearing, why had she stopped? Why not heal *all* the trees—bring the whole forest back to life? Before Bibi could ask, Corineus went on. "The Quickening is what she called her magic. She said she would heal the rest of the forest, and she *will*. We just have to wait. She's out there. She must know you're here. She'll show herself, soon. You'll see."

Soon? Soon wasn't . . . well, soon enough. Bibi wanted her

mom to show herself *now*. She had helped the elk, and she would help Bibi. She would make the hylophobia go away.

Still—why had she gone into the dead forest, where the lions were? Bibi stared at the sea of black trees for a long time, arms crossed, squeezing herself tight—as Corineus closed his eyes, easing down to his underside in the grass, looking almost cat-like with his thin legs folding beneath him.

Eek, Mom—where are *you?*

CHAPTER NINETEEN:
Home

The rest of the day passed slowly. Under the bright, clear sky, the air stayed hot like the kiln in the art room at school—making Bibi sticky and woozy. Only once did she and Corineus change positions, to gather blackberries on the lee side of the hill—after which they returned to sit and wait at the summit.

By mid-afternoon, the elk in the clearing below began practice-fighting. "In case the lions ever get in," Corineus said, watching them. Genza, Zezo, and Baranji charged at one another, smacking their stubby, velvety antlers together, like the boys Bibi used to see in peewee football after school. Yega-Woo and Aruna kicked violently into the air a few times, and then Yega-Woo led everyone in wind sprints—Bibi could hear her telling them how to lean to one side while skirting an obstacle, how to find running rhythm, how to build momentum.

"My sister is the fastest elk in the forest," Corineus said, his chest swelling a bit.

"Why don't you go practice with them?" Bibi said, putting the last of the blackberries in her mouth. Her hands were smudged with the obsidian-colored juice, and she wiped them on her jeans, and then moved to sit cross-legged. "I can wait for Mom by myself."

"My antlers haven't come yet," Corineus said, his voice shrinking before he blew his tuft of hair out of his eyes. "I try to grow them every day. But they won't come." His voice faltered. "Zezo and Baranji will laugh at me. *Runt*, they call me."

Bibi winced. She knew what that felt like. *You won't believe what she's scared of.*

"Yega-Woo won't laugh at you," she said, thinking of how tender the doe had been with her little brother. "And I don't think Aruna or Genza will, either."

Corineus broke into a rare smile. "We used to live *there*," he said, and pointed with his nose to a faraway patch of Falanthrow Forest—a blackness upon the black, barely visible from the hill. "Splitwood—our home."

"Splitwood?" Bibi squinted, pushing her glasses higher on her nose. "Why do you call it that?" As best she could tell, the clearing was nearer to one side of the dead forest, while the faraway patch made a bullseye in the middle.

"There is a two-trunked tree there," Corineus said, eyes still fixed on the distant blot. "The River Eldred is nearby—on hot days, we swam in it to cool off."

Oh, a swim would feel good today. Bibi's neck prickled with

the sting of sunburn, as another flurry of gnats flitted around her head. She shooed them away, into the parched grass.

"Where is *your* home, Bibi Blundermuss?" Corineus said, turning to her. "Where did you come from?"

Bibi furrowed her brow. "Didn't my mom tell you?"

He shook his head. She thought for a moment. If only she could talk to her dad, with his telescope and star charts—he'd know how to explain this. Home was so far away. And here at the other end of the Cosmos, it was so complicated.

"Um," she began. Should she tell Corineus about Oregon? She loved it there—but could she call it *home*? It hadn't felt that way for six months, with her parents gone. But even before . . . Bibi rubbed her chin, remembering a discussion from the first day of class that year. "Where's your family from?" Ms. MacTavish had asked the students. Everyone else's families had been in Oregon for generations. Bibi's had been there only two years—and before that, five years in Los Angeles. And before that? All she knew was that their families came from two places—her mom's from South Africa, her dad's from Denmark. Strange countries, near the top and bottom of the Earth.

"You can't come from *two* places," Ellery Finley had whispered after she shared. "That's like coming from no place at all."

On High Hill, Corineus still waited for an answer. Bibi frowned. Her parents had kept so much about their past—*her* past—secret. What should she say? Where *was* her home?

"I come from somewhere beautiful," she said at last. She

told him of Oregon's green everywhere—even in the gray sky and blue rain. Green in the black of the high desert night, in the dirt and wood, in the wind and sea, and in the mountains formed in slow-motion by slabs of slipping rock.

Corineus gave her a longing look. "And no Trolliclawians? That sounds perfect!"

By sunset, the five other elk youngsters made their way to High Hill, chatting and joking. Bibi began to worry that maybe her mom wouldn't show herself today. Maybe the Quickening wouldn't come after all?

But then how long would she have to wait?

Soon the elk gathered in a circle on the hilltop—the bucks' stubby antlers reminding her of hand shadow-puppets in the twilight. When the sun sank, night dropped quickly, like a black curtain—darkness so complete at first that Bibi felt like she had returned to outer space. It made her realize her exhaustion— body aching from the long journey across the Cosmos.

"What about my mom?" she whispered to Corineus, as she tried to find a comfortable place to lay down in the grass. The others chatted in the darkness, and the stars began to blink on, one by one. "What about the Quickening?"

She couldn't see Corineus's face, but she heard the disappointment in his voice. "The Quickening will come tomorrow, Bibi Blundermuss. I just know it will."

A phosphorescent yellow-green plant grew among the

grasses of the hilltop—the elk called it *Photinus foliosa*. Under the night sky, its firefly-light made the hilltop pulse with the incandescence of a late-night garden party—just enough to see by.

Hold on, Mom, Bibi thought. *Hold on, Eek and Dad.*

Genza deemed the order of the night watch. Each elk would guard the hill in turn—in case the lions somehow broke through the ring of living trees in the night. Genza recited the watchers' names. "Aruna will go first. Then Baranji, Zezo, Yega-Woo . . ."

Before Bibi heard more, she was asleep.

CHAPTER TWENTY:
Another Message

The Quickening did not come the next day, or the day after that. Bibi's hylophobia dwindled—only to be replaced by the anxiety of waiting. The days on High Hill were long and hot, with not much to do but eat berries, refill her water bottle from a brook that bubbled up near the base of the hill, and watch the elk practice.

All the while, she kept coming back to the same questions. Where was her mom? Where was Eek? And was her dad here, too?

Her nightmares grew fainter—echoes of the ones at home. The trees still chased her in them—with their long grasping arms, and their awful *tok, tok, tok*—but in slow motion. Bibi always woke before getting caught—calling for Eek before remembering she was gone.

How many days would Eek have to wander the dead forest with the white lions? Sometimes Bibi paced the summit of High Hill, listening hard for her little black cat's small meow under the wind-chime pollen and the chattering of the cicadas. It never came.

At least Eek had a disguise. What had the Trolliclawians called her? *Black catling.* They thought she was one of them.

How long before they found out she wasn't?

On the morning of the fourth day, Bibi woke from her nightmare with a start. She sat up. From her spot on High Hill, she saw that the sun had stretched its first light across the sky, not yet reaching down past the mountains surrounding the forest. The clearing lay in shadow, and the air was crisp. She rubbed her side, sore from sleeping on the ground.

She put her glasses on and checked her pockets. In one, the photograph of her parents—two daredevils—worn and water-stained, but still there. In the other, her phone. She wondered if the battery had any life left at all.

The young elk were still asleep, scattered across the hill's far slope. Breath visible in the air, Bibi pulled her denim jacket closer, and rubbed her hands for warmth. Below, the living trees seemed to create their own light in the dim dawn, sleepily releasing the first pollen of the day—pure, like the first breath of a newborn. But beyond that, Falanthrow Forest appeared as a void—scorched and black and barren. Bibi shuddered.

Something flashed among the black trees.

She blinked. Had she imagined that? The afterimage floated across her retinas, like someone had just taken her photo without warning. Quickly, hands trembling, she removed her glasses, wiped them, put them back on, and leaned forward.

Yes! There! No longer a flash, though—a patch of light in the dead forest. It faded to a warm glow as she watched.

A small, distant section of Falanthrow Forest—hard to tell how big from here, maybe the size of a city block, and maybe a few miles away—shimmered with red-orange light. Red-orange like the remote bonfires she had seen down the beach on that Oregon Coast trip. Red-orange like . . . the color of Falanthrow flowers.

Bibi knew what this had to be. The faraway trees, like the ones around the clearing, had come alive. The Quickening!

"Corineus!" she said.

With a grunt and a scramble of hooves, the little elk appeared out of the morning murk. "Are you okay, Bibi Blundermuss?" he said—and then he saw, too. He froze.

Bibi reached one arm in front of her until her hand was silhouetted against the shimmering red-orange light—as if she could touch her mom's magic. So close, yet so far. She trembled as the other elk roused themselves, until all were gathered at the top of High Hill.

"She's there," Bibi said, imagining she could feel warmth from the glow—like a hearth fire for a weary traveler. "She's really *there*."

"That's Splitwood!" Yega-Woo said, ears splayed. "She's healing Splitwood!"

Bibi blinked. Yega Woo was right. The center of the forest. The area Corineus had pointed out a few days ago. Their home. No wonder he stood riveted, watching.

"It's *only* Splitwood," Zezo said, shaking dead grass off his brindle coat. "So, it can't be the Quickening. The lions are still out there. What good does another patch of living trees do us?"

"Yeah, what good does it do us?" Baranji said, in a lulling voice.

Bibi's shoulders slumped. The trees in Splitwood had come alive, but Zezo was right—the magic stopped there. The magic had a clear edge. Her mom was *only* healing Splitwood.

"What does it mean, Cori?" Genza said, looking at the little elk.

"I—I don't know," Corineus said.

Bibi knit her brows. *She* should know what it meant. There had to be a reason her mom had chosen those trees. What was it? How could you not know something so important about your own mom?

On her neck, she felt the tingle of sunlight. It had begun to spill into the valley, touching the hill, making the glittery trees around the clearing seem to dance awake. This would be another hot day, Bibi could tell—the rolling chorus of cicada chatter already swelling.

Then, another sound: *buzz.*

Bibi spun around, listening intently. What was that? Immediately she thought of the bees. Had some survived their encounter with Valmyr after all? But she saw nothing. And the buzz was intermittent—not like the bees.

The young elk looked at her, ears rotating like antennae.

Buzz.

Bibi looked down. She dug into her pocket.

Her phone.

The buzz telling her a text had arrived.

A text! How—here at the other end of the Cosmos?

What are you waiting for? she told herself as she frantically reached into her pocket to pull the device out. The elk watched with wide eyes. She studied the phone, unable to believe what she was seeing, and reading and re-reading the name of the sender.

The text had come from her mom.

CHAPTER TWENTY-ONE:
R U Here?

Bibi's hands went jittery as she held her phone.

R U here? the text said.

"What are you doing?" Corineus brought his nose so close that he fogged up the phone's screen. "What's that?"

Bibi wanted to jump and yell—her mom had *texted* her. Impossible! But she saw the message right there, clear as the sunrise.

She saw the confused looks on the elk's faces. They had never seen a phone before. She searched for a way to explain. She could say a phone was like a computer—but they wouldn't understand that, either.

Bibi crinkled her brow, speaking rapidly. "It's a phone. You use it to talk to people, or look things up, or . . . share a picture of your breakfast."

The elk exchanged befuddled glances. Bibi sighed, frustration mounting. Stay focused. Answer the text, quickly. What should she say? She bent over the screen and began typing with her thumbs. The elk's confusion grew as the phone burped tapping noises in time with her fingers.

I'm here! Bibi typed. From the corner of her eye, she noticed the battery life. Three percent. She typed faster. *Where R U?* Send. *Bloop*, the phone said.

The elk smiled at the sound, and Bibi blushed—as soon as the message was sent, she saw the foolishness of the question. *Where R U?* She knew *exactly* where—in the dead part of Falanthrow Forest, in Splitwood, with that little red-orange patch of living trees. Bibi looked up, just to be sure. Yes—right there, still shimmering with magic.

Then she realized something else—if she could text, why didn't she call? "Nobody uses a phone to *talk* anymore," Grandma Ivy used to say, bracelets jangling as she wagged her finger—that's why she had insisted on keeping that old-fashioned one in the downstairs hallway.

Quickly, Bibi dialed her mom's number.

"Are you sending the Arbor Guardian a picture of your breakfast?" Aruna said.

"Shh!" Bibi said, as the phone rang on the other end. Why hadn't she thought of this sooner? Why hadn't she called right away? *Ring.* Well, for one thing, she couldn't expect a call to go through at the wrong end of the Cosmos. But she'd figure that out later. *Ring.* Bibi's hand shook so much she thought she might drop the phone.

She heard a click, and a voice on the other end.

"Acorn?" Nan Blundermuss said.

For a second, Bibi couldn't speak. She felt herself grow light—like she had turned into a balloon, tugging at its string, ready to lift into the summer sky. *Mom.*

And then her phone died.

CHAPTER TWENTY-TWO:
A Lighthouse

"Mom?" Bibi yelled, as her imagined balloon popped. "*Mom!*"
She looked at the blank screen and the spinning circle telling
her of the battery draining away. She squeezed the phone, barely
resisting the urge to throw it into the grass. "No no no no *NO!*"

The elk backed away from her as if surprised by her anger.

Bibi bit her lip, blinking back tears. Her mom's voice. She
had heard her mom's voice. Not from the bees, but her *real* voice,
right there on the phone. It had been six months since she last
heard that voice. It was like hearing from a ghost.

"It was *her*," she said, agony and love tumbled up inside.
"She's really here."

Zezo grumbled dismissively. He turned back to the red-
orange patch of forest. "But what is she *doing*?"

"Yes, *what*?" Baranji said.

No one answered. Bibi wiped her eyes, beginning to understand. *R U here?* A memory stirred. The Oregon Coast trip. *Do you know what that's for, Acorn? Signaling people who are far away.* They had been passing a windy inlet, where her mom pointed to . . .

"A lighthouse," Bibi said now, in a hush.

The young elk looked even more confused. "What?" Genza said.

Bibi put her phone back in her pocket, thinking. "A lighthouse. A *lighthouse!*" She turned to the others and smiled for the first time in days. "She's signaling me, don't you see? She wants me to know where she is." Excitement crested in her like the waves on that coast trip. She grabbed her backpack and slung it over her shoulder. "I have to go to Splitwood."

The elk's eyes immediately widened.

"What about the Trolliclawians!" Aruna said.

Bibi looked at Corineus. His expression asked a different question: *What about the trees?*

She shook her head, hard—like shaking her nightmare away. She had known this moment would come. She couldn't let the hylophobia stop her—her mom was right *there*. At last Bibi could follow through on the whole reason for being here. She set her jaw. She would fight her fear, like before—*better* than before. She had to try. She would find her mom. Her mom would know where Eek and Dad were. Her mom would make the hylophobia go away. Then they would all go home.

Yes. She turned to the others and, not knowing what else to do, bowed awkwardly.

90

"Goodbye!"

She began walking down the hill, swinging her arms. But before she had taken ten steps, Corineus called out after her.

"Wait, Bibi Blundermuss!" She stopped, and he moved to stand next to her, turning to face his fellows, resolutely. "I'm sorry—I can't let her go by herself. I'm going, too."

The older elk looked at him as if he had said he would start flying. They shifted in place, ears batting at the heat. The chatter of cicadas rolled across the hill.

Finally, Genza spoke, quietly. "I know you've been out there already, Cori. And we're proud of you for it. But this? This is unwise. You were lucky. The forest is not safe, eh?" He looked at Bibi. "Neither of you should go."

Only Zezo seemed unfazed. With an uncharacteristically contemplative expression, he turned to Genza.

"Actually—Runt is right. We should *all* go."

Genza raised a brow as the others murmured.

"Oh, I don't agree with his reasons," Zezo continued. "You know I don't trust the Arbor Guardian. But we can't keep running from the Trolliclawians. This is our chance to show them we aren't scared—that we can fight back. If Valmyr and his lions have surrounded Nan Blundermuss, they won't be expecting us to come at them from behind." He looked at the others and grinned severely. "Antlers and hooves will beat the white lions."

"Why does it matter if Valmyr and his lions won't be expecting us?" Genza said, with a sidelong glance at Zezo. "What about *other* lions, eh?"

Zezo did not respond. Bibi looked at Corineus. "You don't

have to come," she said. She couldn't delay. Who knew how long that glowing patch of forest would be there? She turned to go.

"I'm not afraid," Corineus said, following her.

"Wait!" Genza said, frustration mounting in his voice. Bibi stopped again. Genza looked at Yega-Woo searchingly. "What do you think, Sweet Yega-Woo? About going with them, I mean?"

Bibi crossed her arms, trying to keep her impatience at bay. She did not want to endanger the elk. But again—if they were going, they had to go *now*. While her mom was still there.

Yega-Woo, deep in thought, wrinkled her nose. "I don't want Cori to go without me." She looked at her brother, standing taller. "I will help him protect Bibi Blundermuss."

Seeming surprised, Genza slowly turned to Aruna. The copper doe chose her words carefully. "Maybe there are other elk still out there. Maybe we'll find them if we go."

What about Baranji? Bibi saw him look away, as if hoping they wouldn't notice him. Feeling their attention, he met their eyes reluctantly.

"Antlers and hooves will beat the white lions," he said at last—but Bibi thought she heard a catch in his slow voice.

Genza *humph*ed, and then laughed—taken off-guard by how quickly the plan had formed. He brandished his stubby antlers from side to side. He turned back to Bibi.

"Well, then, I guess it's settled, eh? We're going with you, Bibi Blundermuss."

Bibi kept her eyes on the red-orange patch of Splitwood trees as she and the elk hiked down High Hill. The sun rose, turning the grass from brown to gold. When they finally got to the bottom of the hill, they could no longer see beyond the living trees that surrounded the clearing, and Splitwood disappeared from view.

Bibi breathed deep as they walked across the field. This was it. She did not actually *want* to go into Falanthrow Forest again. But she meant it when she said she *had* to. How long would her mom's signal last?

She wiped the sweat from the back of her neck. She wanted to take her jacket off—but soon they would be in the mist, and everything would be cooler.

"The journey to Splitwood will take all morning," Genza said from out in front, as they made their way across the clearing. "Yega-Woo and I will lead. Follow us and move quietly, eh? We'll go slow to avoid ambushes. Remain alert in the mist—you know how it hides the white lions."

Zezo grunted toward Corineus. "Do you really want to come, Runt? No offense, but without antlers—"

"Unlike you, Zezo," Corineus said, "I've already been out there by myself."

Zezo shrugged.

In a few minutes they were at the first of the living trees—and there, everyone paused. Legs shaking, Bibi breathed in the gingery scent of the Falanthrow pollen and wiped her moist palms on her jeans.

In the growing light of morning, the elk stared as the trees released a glittery shower of pollen. Bibi had to turn away—it sparkled so bright it seemed to scorch her eyes. But that wasn't all—she felt her hylophobia moving inside, like a snake stirring in her belly. Like it had been waiting for this moment.

Corineus looked up at her, with eyes that seemed to say, *Are you sure?* She nodded, grateful he had kept her forest-fear a secret. What would the others think if they knew?

Zezo's brindle coat bristled. "Well, what are we waiting for? Let's go."

"Antlers and hooves will beat the white lions!" Genza said.

"Antlers and hooves will beat the white lions!" the others repeated. "Huzzah, huzzah!"

And with that, they entered the forest.

CHAPTER TWENTY-THREE:
Back to the Trees

It took only a few minutes to pass through the ring of living trees.

Then, just like that, they were back in the dead forest, on a dirt trail that had been worn over time by many hooves. It seemed like another world here—still and stale. Bibi felt the air cooling on her face. She looked behind her at the last few living trees. They sent down a farewell burst of pollen, accompanied by the tinkling wind-chime sound.

Zezo, the last of the group, scowled at her. "Keep moving, daughter of Nan Blundermuss."

The hylophobia began to gnaw at her insides, as much as it had on that first terrible day. The black trees. The smell of sour soil. Shoving her hands deep in her jacket pockets, Bibi felt a lurch of queasiness. Her head spun. She remembered what her book had said—a seizure would be next, if she wasn't careful. *Inhale, exhale.* She had to control this.

How strange to be scared of trees even though your mom was a tree witch! What would Ms. MacTavish have called it? Oh, yeah: *irony.* Like when Ellery Finley had spent all week teasing Cassandra Platt about how she pronounced the word "bedraggled"—she emphasized the syllable "bed"—only to miss that word on the vocabulary test.

Bibi looked up but could no longer see the sun.

"Bibi Blundermuss," Corineus whispered. Walking parallel with her on the narrow path, he tilted his head until the hair tuft moved out of his eyes. "Are you okay? Do you want to get on my back and ride for a while?"

Bibi smiled as best she could. "I'm fine," she said.

But in truth, not much time passed before she wanted to give up. Feeling this bad just a little way in, she didn't know how she'd make it all the way to Splitwood. The journey would take all morning, Genza had said. Bibi's frustration quickly became overwhelming. They were about to find her mom, at last—shouldn't she be able to do the thing she had come here to do? The thing she wanted most of all? It was so unfair!

She thought she might swoon. She gritted her teeth. *Don't have a seizure.* She could handle the nausea and dizziness for a bit longer, but not a seizure. And she didn't want the others to see her struggle. Especially Corineus. She held her breath, trying to make the bad feeling pass. She needed to concentrate on something else, like before.

But what? The path tapered, forcing them all into a single

file. Bibi followed Corineus as he stepped carefully around a root, black and coiled like Eek's tail.

Eek's tail . . . Eek . . . *Sawubona, Eek.* What else had Mom and Grandma Ivy said about *sawubona*? Not just "good day"—it meant something more, right?

Bibi rubbed her eyes under her glasses, trying to remember. She could hardly see with all this mist. To see . . .

Wait. *I see you.* That's what *sawubona* really meant, right?

She frowned, holding her stomach as she walked. No. Not *I* see you. *We* see you. She had been too young to understand *sawubona* before. But somehow, here at the other end of the Cosmos, lost and on her own, trying to distract herself from her fear, needing her mom's help more than ever, the word began to make sense. For the first time, she felt its weight, like a smooth old stone in her hand. *We see you.* You exist, and you're where you're supposed to be. Could that be how it felt to belong—to know everything would be all right, and you no longer had to be scared?

Maybe someday, Bibi would feel that too.

Ahead of her, Genza and Yega-Woo paused, and the line of elk stopped without saying a word. Bibi hitched up her backpack and waited. They had come to a fork in the path. Genza and Yega-Woo whispered back and forth.

After a moment, they chose the left side of the fork and moved on, deeper into the dead forest.

CHAPTER TWENTY-FOUR:
Splitwood

As Genza had predicted, it took all morning to follow the path to Splitwood. Along the way, they did not see the white lions or even detect their scent. Several times Genza and the other bucks paused to strip the velvet from their antlers—scraping it against the black trees and revealing the sharp spiked prongs that had been hidden underneath. The mist hung everywhere in the air. The tedious light filtering through reminded Bibi of the basement at school, with its cold, dim fluorescent bulbs.

The elk moved silently, like drifting smoke. Bibi kept silent, too. But in her mind, she wrestled with her hylophobia at every step—each one a bit harder than the last. Her stomach strained and contorted. Her heart beat like a jackhammer as she jumped from thought to thought, trying to stay ahead of her fear. Corineus looked back at her occasionally—always with concern in his eyes. Each time, she found the strength to reassure him with a wave. How long could she keep doing that?

Don't think of the trees, she told herself over and over. *Don't think of the trees. Think of something else. Think of things you like.*

Playing the wind chimes.

The trip to the Museum of Natural History.

The trip to the Oregon Coast.

Books to read next year, in eighth grade.

How about smaller things?

Genza's antlers, freed of their velvet. Corineus's hair tuft, bobbing with his steps. Yega-Woo's eyes, bright in their blackness, even in the misty gloom. Zezo, in back, glaring fiercely into the forest, his brindle coat bristling. Bibi folded her arms across her chest and tried her best to look fierce too.

She heard a faint noise. She shut her eyes for a moment, listening deeper. Far away. A concentrated babbling. The chatter of . . . running water.

She opened her eyes. Running water? Before she could ask, the elk stopped again.

Bibi did not want to stay here. The hylophobia got worse when she stood still—it got harder to distract herself. She needed to keep moving. She felt the forest start to twirl around her slowly—she reached out to steady herself against Corineus.

"Why did we stop?"

Corineus shifted uneasily. "We're in the center of the forest," he said, his nostrils flaring, his ears rotating like satellite dishes. "We're in Splitwood." He pointed his nose toward a two-trunked tree in the path ahead. "That's the Splitwood tree. Do you hear the River Eldred?"

The two-trunked tree. The running water. Bibi shook her head. How could this be Splitwood? She saw no sign of the Quickening.

"Shouldn't these trees be alive?"

Genza looked around—and Bibi, even in her dizziness, saw uncertainty in his eyes. Holding her stomach, she tried to massage the fear and discomfort away. A horrible thought came—what if her mom already left, taking her magic with her? What if there were no living Falanthrows here after all—after coming all this way? What if Bibi had completely misinterpreted her mom's signal? Leading her friends into a . . . trap?

Another noise sounded. Someone moved up ahead—toward the group, out in the mist, slow clopping on the hard path. Bibi's breath came faster, and she felt a chill. Not lions—too noisy. Not her mom, either.

"Be ready," Zezo said to the group, jaw tightening. The elk's muscles spasmed as they leaned toward the approaching noise.

Three strangers—disheveled elk stags—limped out of the mist.

CHAPTER TWENTY-FIVE:
The Strangers

The strange stags looked hungry—thin and brittle, almost like stick figures. They were old, and their antlers ranged larger than Genza's, but with pockmarks and chips. A sleepless look guttered in their eyes. They seemed not to see the younger elk until nearly upon them—when they came to a clumsy stop in front of the two-trunked tree.

It took a moment before anyone spoke. Yega-Woo broke the silence first, her voice an astonished whisper. "Fathers—we didn't know there were other elk in the forest. We are so happy to see you." She bowed.

The leader of the strangers turned to her, face gaunt as withered wood. "You shouldn't be here, girl. Lions are coming."

Lions? Bibi tensed. She felt her companions bracing, looking to either side of the path for any sign of trouble, but finding none.

Genza dropped his voice. "What do you mean, sir?" he said. "There's no scent here, eh?"

The gaunt stag laughed—a dry, forced sound, thrown out like a handful of sand.

"Do you think they will *warn* you when they come, boy?"

Yega-Woo looked at Genza, then back at the strangers. "We're searching for the Arbor Guardian, Fathers. Have you seen her?"

The gaunt stag wrinkled his brow, as Genza scanned the misty forest again, inhaling deeply through his nose. Heart beating as if it would punch out of her, Bibi followed his gaze. Nothing moved among the trees, but that did not lessen her fear. She squeezed the straps of her backpack tight and braced herself to run.

"I don't know any 'Arbor Guardian,'" the gaunt stag said, a disconcerting dullness in his voice. "All I know is what I said before: you shouldn't be here. If you stay here, you will die."

Zezo sneered. "Die? Not us, Old One. Not today."

Stout Baranji gave a lethargic grin, until Genza shot them both a glare, and then turned to the strangers again.

"If you help us find the Arbor Guardian, we can take you somewhere safe—protected by living trees, eh?"

The gaunt stag laughed again, but with more bite. Bibi began to think he didn't want their help. "There are no living trees, son!" he said, bitterly. "We should know—we have traveled the whole forest since the Harrowing began."

"There's a clearing, Fathers!" Yega-Woo said. "Small enough to miss, but big enough for all of us, and with a ring of living trees around it. Just half a day south of here! It's protected and safe, thanks to the Arbor Guardian. That's why we're trying to find her. She can heal the whole forest and drive the white lions out."

The gaunt stag's smile faded. "If you believe that, you're bigger fools than I thought." He looked at his comrades, and then back to the youngsters. "But it's no concern of ours. Step aside and let us pass. The lions will find you soon enough."

"I told you—we don't fear the lions!" Zezo said. "We can fight back."

"Quiet, Zezo!" Genza said.

Bibi thought she saw the gaunt stag's expression turn a shade darker. Even in the frailty of old age, he seemed to rise up a little—glaring at the younger elk like a stern parent.

"You want to go to *war* with the Trolliclawians? Ha! You're not looking for the Arbor Guardian—you're looking for the Alala."

Bibi's companions shifted in place. "The Alala?" Genza said. "What's that?"

The stag huffed. "Other survivors, son. Warrior elk. A whole herd, in the northern part of the forest. They are young, and strong, and stupid. They too think they can beat the lions."

Warrior elk? Bibi tried to imagine a whole herd of Zezos.

"But what about the old saying?" Genza said. "Antlers and hooves—"

"—will get you killed," the stag said. "Join them if you wish. Now, as I said: *step aside.*"

Genza looked stung. Bibi rubbed her shoulder—whoever these "Alala" were, she couldn't believe the strangers would turn down a chance to join them—or to join Genza and Yega-Woo. Wouldn't there be safety in numbers?

Finally, after a glance at Yega-Woo, Genza sighed, and stepped out of the way, letting the strangers pass. As they left, Zezo scowled, muttering under his breath, too soft for the elder stags to hear:

"We'll see who the biggest fools are, Old Ones."

Bibi shivered. And just like that, the three strangers vanished into the mist.

CHAPTER TWENTY-SIX:
Nowhere Left to Wander

If you stay here, you will die. The gaunt stag's words kept repeating in Bibi's head. She began shaking uncontrollably.

With the strangers gone, the young elk exchanged glances in the thick mist.

"The Arbor Guardian can't have gone far," Genza said. "Let's find her, quickly."

Silently, cautiously, they moved forward. Ten steps; twenty. At first, nothing changed. The same black, dead trees. The same mist.

But soon, an awful new scent drifted near. Bibi, already ill with hylophobia, gagged—her throat burning. She knew this scent. She thought back to her first day in Falanthrow Forest. The scent of the white lions. Blood, iron, urine, and bile. *The Trolliclawians are here.*

Had the lions *captured* her mom? The thought made Bibi's skin crawl.

"We should leave," Aruna whispered. "It's not safe."

"It's too late," Yega-Woo said. "Circle up—protect Cori and Bibi Blundermuss."

Without argument, the young elk stopped and made an outward-facing circle—Genza, Yega-Woo, Aruna, Zezo, and Baranji in a ring, with Corineus and Bibi in the middle. "Get on, Bibi Blundermuss," Corineus whispered.

Bibi's chest hurt with her throbbing heart. She wrapped her arms around Corineus's neck and pulled herself up. She watched the others scan the forest, their muscles tensing. She couldn't tell where the lion scent was coming from. Everyone shifted in place, as if balancing between caution and panic.

"We should *leave*," Aruna said again, her voice shaking as it rose. "We should run!"

"No!" Zezo said. Unable to wait, he broke away from the others, and began cantering around them, with a strange sound like a snarl, hooves pounding in the dead leaves. "Show yourselves, Trolliclawian scum!" he called out toward the black trees, body hunched like a street fighter in an alley, antlers like two daggers on top of his head, ready to cut any who came at him. "Or are you *scared?*"

"Zezo—quiet!" Genza said in a hush. "Get back with the group!"

Panic prickled across Bibi's skin. Had Zezo gone mad? He would give them away!

"Come on, Genza!" the brindle buck said, continuing to circle. "Stand up—fight back. Let's not hide anymore."

The wretched feline odor became overpowering. Bibi covered her nose with her denim sleeve but couldn't shut the awfulness out. Zezo stopped suddenly—staring at something.

Too late to run. Did a Trolliclawian's shadow lurk in the mist behind that tree? No—Bibi thought her eyes must be playing tricks on her.

Wait—*yes*. She wanted to shriek.

The Trolliclawians are here.

Five long shadows moved around the elk in the swirling white. Bibi could barely make them out—but she saw enough to make her blood drain, and her mouth dry.

Mist-colored, silent, and huge—nearly as tall as the elk, and twice as long from nose to tail—the lions circled closer. Close enough that Bibi felt their breath, hot and ferric. Saw their coats, flecked with blood. Saw their ears, pointed like short sharp horns.

Pollen from the Falanthrow trees is deadly to the Trolliclawians, Bibi reminded herself, head spinning with fear, stomach wrenching. *Mom, where are you?* There was no sign of her—or Eek. But Bibi recognized some of the lions from before. Gorka, the bruiser. Alenka, the sleek white-gold lioness. And a flash of red teeth in the mist.

"It seems the wanderers have nowhere left to wander," Valmyr said, voice oozing out like lava. He signaled, and

the lions stopped circling. They sat back on their haunches, gracefully wrapping their tails about them, fixing their prey with expressions of infinite patience.

Bibi hardly dared breathe. Somewhere out of the corner of her eye, she sensed a lingering leaf on one of the dead Falanthrows, as it separated from its branch, and fluttered with excruciating slowness to the ground. What were the lions waiting for? But she knew. Eek had done this with spiders and ants. Savoring the kill—drawing it out.

Bibi forced herself to breathe slowly. The pain in her stomach became unbearable.

Genza snorted violently and lowered his antlers—two barbed pikes—toward Valmyr. Would that even work? Could the elk harm the lions at all? The Trolliclawians slatted their eyes and leaned forward ever-so-slightly—no more than a tree leans forward in a wind. They bared their teeth to the gums.

"I know you, don't I, woodskull?" Valmyr said, turning his yellow eyes to Genza's antlers, and then his scar.

Woodskull. Bibi finally understood the term. As if a tree grew from Genza's head.

Nearby, the river kept babbling. Valmyr flexed his claws, raking them in the dirt. Then he noticed Bibi. She swallowed hard.

"And you!" Valmyr said. He must have remembered her from the day she arrived. She flattened herself against Corineus's trembling back—her fear a venom suffusing her blood. She tried to make herself as small as a bird, or a bee—she wished she could fly away. She wished she had never come here. She wished . . .

Before anyone could stop him, Zezo lunged at Gorka, spiky antlers low.

CHAPTER TWENTY-SEVEN:
Zezo's Stand

The group exploded with violence. The does kicked powerfully. The bucks stabbed with sharp antlers. Corineus staggered, turning in place as the circle of elk closed around him defensively. Dizzy and desperate with hylophobia and fear, Bibi saw only chaos. The lions attacked everywhere—a white whirlwind of teeth and claws that kept coming. They painted red stripes on the elk hides.

"Zezo!" Genza shouted.

Bibi turned. Zezo had broken from the chaos, and drawn Gorka and Alenka with him, away from the other elk. Bibi feared they would kill him right away, but he did a ferocious pirouette—twisting, kicking, and stabbing in all directions at once, so quickly that his attackers couldn't get at him. Soon their white fur was splotched with scarlet. They panted angrily, trying to keep up.

Zezo held Gorka and Alenka off for so long that Valmyr and the other two lions stopped their assault, watching. Flashing a manic grin, Zezo shouted at his attackers. "Are we supposed to be scared of *you?*" he said. "Miserable sacks of skin and bones— that's what you are!"

"Zezo!" Genza said through clenched teeth. "Get out of there!"

All the lions seethed, attention locked on the frenzy of the brindle-coated elk and his mocking laugh.

From the corner of her eye, Bibi saw a blur of white. Valmyr moved like a missile over the forest floor, shooting between his comrades. Before Bibi could blink, he tackled Zezo from the side, slicing his neck open with a sweep of his paw.

No!

Poor Zezo toppled like an old tree struck by lightning, blood pouring out from under his jaw. Gorka and Alenka skirted back as he fell—watching as the side of his head thudded against a boulder. Aruna gave a small yelp.

On the ground, Zezo convulsed, and kicked, and groaned as he bled out. Then he stopped moving.

NO!

Dead. Zezo—dead.

Valmyr spun around to face the other elk, wiping his claws in the dirt.

"This is the fate of those who challenge Lord Valmyr, King of the Trolliclawians!" he spat, raising his paw and brandishing his diamond-sharp claws. "Who's next?"

Bibi felt Corineus's small frame jittering beneath her. Then

111

she noticed something else. As the lions had moved to watch Valmyr's attack, they left space open in the circle. Space enough for an elk to run through.

CHAPTER TWENTY-EIGHT:
Go!

Yega-Woo had seen it too.

"*Go!*" she cried, leaping into the breach—and quick as a thunderclap, Genza, Aruna, and Baranji followed her, eyes rolled back and white. Corineus sprang after them so abruptly that Bibi nearly slipped from her perch.

"Get them!" Valmyr said.

Throwing off the euphoria of first-kill, the lions gave chase, like a squad of vengeful demons. Baranji and Aruna took an open path; but Yega-Woo followed an intricately twisted one, with low brush. Genza and Corineus ran behind her as best they could. What had Corineus said? His sister—the fastest elk in the forest. Bibi could hardly hold on—her knuckles turning white as she grasped the little elk's fur, her glasses sliding down her nose.

She used the crook of her elbow to push them up, desperately trying to see. Why had Aruna and Baranji gone a different direction? Shouldn't they all stick together? She shuddered and tried to shake away the horrible memory of Zezo on the ground, in a pool of his own blood, skull cracked, eyes empty.

She looked behind her. The other lions must have turned after Aruna and Baranji. Only Valmyr dared follow the fastest elk in the forest, through the convoluted path, with long, strong strides—echoing every twist and turn, as if he could read Yega-Woo's mind. His paws beat out a dull *pata-thump* on the forest floor.

"I *do* know you, woodskull!" Valmyr shouted at Genza. "And this time I'm going to kill you! I'm going to kill all of you!"

Yega-Woo moved like ricocheting lightning between the dead trees, Genza and Corineus doing their best to keep up. On Corineus's back, Bibi hunkered down. Her head spun as the three elk moved one way, then the next—turn, sprint, turn, sprint. She heard Genza's gruff breath. The white mist cloaked everything—hiding each cluster of trees until they were upon it. But Yega-Woo ran fast and sure-footed as ever—as if back in the clearing, racing through open grass.

Pata-thump, pata-thump, pata-THUMP! came the red-toothed lion's paws behind them, louder and harder.

The three elk skittered to one side—nearly losing control—leaping over a log, one after the other. All three got low, scrambling under drooping branches, along a culvert, and up to a flat area where the trees were even denser.

Still Valmyr crashed through behind them, getting closer each second.

114

They came upon a straightaway and followed it. Corineus, gasping for air, began to lag, and Bibi felt the hot lion breath on her back, turning in time to see Valmyr swipe at her friend with a slab-like paw. He missed, but his yellow eyes briefly locked on Bibi. In them, she saw a heart burning with bloodlust. *I'm going to kill all of you*, they reminded her.

Valmyr swung again, and a crimson stripe appeared on Corineus's haunch. He fishtailed but kept running. "Cori!" Bibi cried, though she knew her words wouldn't reach him above the sound of the rushing wind, and the hooves, and the paws.

Genza, just ahead, looked back, fury in his face as he labored to match Yega-Woo's pace. "Come *on*, Cori!" he said. "We're almost there!"

Almost where?

Yega-Woo and Genza pulled even farther ahead, until Bibi feared they would be hidden by the mist. Behind her, Valmyr ran so close that she could see the flaring of his nostrils, the long whiskers flat against his cheeks, the thorn-shaped slits that stood in the middle of each eye. She wished she was brave enough to lunge at that face—to scratch the eyes or tear at the whiskers!

Valmyr swiped a third time. More blood stripes appeared on Corineus's hide.

NO!

Then, without warning, they crashed into a snarl of branches, stiff and twisted and brambly. The dead wood tore at Bibi's clothes and hair. A hedge of petrified Falanthrows.

I'm touching tree I'm touching tree I'm touching tree.

115

The hylophobia came cleaving back, nausea and dizziness as merciless as a hard-swung axe. Corineus tried to slam to a halt, as the branches scraped and scratched—but then everything changed, and Bibi felt totally, inexplicably weightless.

In the terrifying half-second that followed, she understood. Unable to stop running, Corineus had launched out from a high, tree-covered bank, arcing through the air like a wounded Pegasus. Then they plunged into the frigid water of the River Eldred with a loud, hard splash.

CHAPTER TWENTY-NINE:
The River Eldred

Water everywhere. Cold everywhere.

Sinking into the river, Bibi couldn't breathe or see. It moved all around her—an endless green murk with no top or bottom. She seized up. *Cori!* She kicked, feeling nothing but current. *Swim!*

She exhaled everything, arcing her arms through the water. Up. Must get up—must get air. Her sodden backpack weighed her down—she squirmed out of it, and the river pulled it away.

Her lungs ached, ravenous for oxygen. Must get up—must get air. She kicked and climbed through the watery darkness until it thinned. Then she broke through the river's surface, gulping and spitting in the noisy gush.

"Bibi Blundermuss!"

Corineus! His thin scared voice, nearly drowned out by

gurgling chop, came from in front of her somewhere. Bibi squinted, trying to see through water-streaked glasses. A wet silhouette on a lower bank, Corineus stood upstream from where they had leapt in. She paddled forward, with the undertow, and in a moment felt the mud and rocks beneath her. Crab-walking along the bank's green slime, she crawled out at last, coughing and wiping the cold silt from her skin.

Corineus stood still among rushes almost as tall as he was. His blood-striped haunches juddered with pain. What was he looking at? Where were Yega-Woo and Genza? Where was Valmyr? The cool air chilled Bibi through her wet clothes.

She followed Corineus's gaze, and her heart sank, like a cinder block dropped into the churning river.

No, no, no, no.

Some fifty feet in front of them, on the sandy riverbank, young Genza stood cornered by Valmyr against a scarp. Neither seemed aware of Yega-Woo nearby—crouched among the tall rushes, watching, river-rock eyes glistening with panic.

"I told you I would get you this time, woodskull," Valmyr said, breathing heavily.

Genza stabbed low with his antlers. Valmyr parried, and then struck up with one paw, opening a seam across the elk's side, very near his scar, and deftly pulling back again, out of range of the hooves. Genza staggered, blood showering out.

Bibi's tongue went dry—she looked at Corineus, but no words came. She looked at Yega-Woo. An aura of fury and fear seemed to crackle around the doe.

"Genza!" Corineus said in a hush. "Oh, Genza!"

"And now to finish you," Valmyr said, and made a noise like a revving motorcycle engine.

But before Valmyr could attack, Yega-Woo charged from the bank and toward him. She slammed into him so hard that he toppled, with a yowl of surprise, and rolled out of the way.

Genza, still stunned by the blow draining his blood, briefly turned toward Yega-Woo with a sinking, distant look. And then, as if overwhelmed by the pain, he collapsed into the wet sand with a sickening thud—unconscious.

Genza!

Yega-Woo had already gone quite a way down the bank—putting a hundred yards or so between her and Valmyr. She stopped to look back as the white lion got to his feet.

Valmyr snarled, tail lashing. "The *doe!*" he said, seeing her and growling, as if he couldn't stand the idea of being bested by a girl.

Bibi understood Yega-Woo's plan—she hoped to distract the king of the white lions, to save Genza from the death blow. But a different understanding appeared in Valmyr's thorn-slit eyes, and he grinned cruelly.

"Is this your—"

Before he had finished his question, Yega-Woo charged down the bank once more and knocked Valmyr sideways into the water. Corineus cried out, softly.

With a clamor, Valmyr righted himself more furiously, leaping back onto the bank and shaking the water off.

"Your mate is as good as dead," he hissed, glancing at the unconscious, bloodied Genza, and then back at Yega-Woo. "And you're next!"

Yega-Woo, standing by the rushes, hardened her eyes. "You will have to catch me, Trolliclawian," she replied. "For I am Yega-Woo, the fastest elk in the forest."

At that, Valmyr exploded with rage, swarming toward her all at once. Quick as a ghost, Yega-Woo flew down the bank again, her white tail vanishing into the white mist. Before Bibi finished her next breath, the elk doe was gone, and Valmyr was gone, both in a cloud of dust—swallowed by the dead forest.

CHAPTER THIRTY:
Onward

Bibi and Corineus scrambled to Genza, still prone in the bloody mud.

"Genza!" Corineus said, tears streaming as he licked at his friend's wound. "Genza!"

On the ground, Genza remained still. Slowly, he opened one bloodshot eye, and then the other—his whole body shaking as consciousness returned. He lifted his head, curling his foam-edged lips into words—his voice an unrecognizable rasp, his face contorted. "Sweet Yega-Woo . . . where is Sweet Yega-Woo?"

"Gone," Corineus said, crying harder. "She's gone, she's gone."

Wound beginning to clot, ribs heaving with his breath, Genza stood, with the determination of one digging himself out of his own grave. "What! What do you mean, Cori?"

Frantically, Bibi tried to think of something she could do to help. "She lured Valmyr away!" she said. "She saved you, Genza. She saved us!"

Genza groaned, dull and primal, as if the news was too much. Then he paused, inhaling through his nose. He spoke again, his voice rising. "Do you smell that?" he said. "*Do you smell that!* That's the Arbor Guardian. She's near! We have to go to her. She can save Yega-Woo, eh?"

"Yes. *Yes!*" Corineus nodded rapidly as Bibi looked around. She couldn't smell anything. But they had been so close to the Quickening when the lions arrived. Her mom *must* be here somewhere. She looked at the paw and hoof prints scattered in the bloody mud. She looked at the mist, hanging like wraiths in the dead trees.

The dead trees—Bibi cringed, feeling her stomach knot. With the lions gone, the hylophobia surged. Worse than before. Worse than ever. Nausea, dizziness, and . . . what would a seizure feel like when it came?

"Can you walk, Genza?" Corineus said.

Genza winced. "Of course. Come on, both of you." Still weak, he pointed with his antlers. "Follow the scent. Let's find the Arbor Guardian. She will fix this. She will make it right. She will make it right."

Bibi, Corineus, and Genza headed west. The Harrowing mist became so heavy that it seemed it might suffocate them. They were so deep in the dead forest—how could Bibi survive this? Only her mom could help her. She dug her fingernails into her palms, hoping the discomfort would distract her. *Inhale, exhale.*

She felt stupid, but she couldn't help wishing she still had her backpack. Grandma Ivy had given it to her for middle school. After the hylophobia came, it had been a comfort in the hallways and on the long bus rides home, as Ellery Finley and the other kids made their fun. And she had put her phone in it after the battery died. That meant her phone was gone too, carried away by the River Eldred.

She almost walked into Corineus when he and Genza stopped abruptly—making themselves still, like the trees. Bibi knew they had seen something bad. She looked out.

Gorka and Alenka were here.

The lions sat together, upwind, a few hundred feet away, in front of a black Falanthrow with a wide crown. They were leaning forward slightly, brows furrowed, studying something so intently that they did not notice the newcomers.

Then Bibi saw another shape—a crumpled figure leaning against the wide-crowned tree. At first, she thought it was a pile of leaves, like people raked in their yards in the fall.

Bibi's breath caught in her throat as the shape stirred. Not a pile of leaves. A woman, sitting cross-legged against the tree, Wellingtons on her feet, a grimy cloak covering the rest of her. She lifted her head to look at the lions with weary, sunken eyes. Her braided shoulder-length hair was slate-gray, and her skin ashy and worn. Bibi felt something clutch at her heart.

"*Mom?*" she whispered.

CHAPTER THIRTY-ONE:
The Arbor Guardian

Bibi wanted to scream. Mom. Mom was *right there*. But so were the lions. If she called out, they might attack. The hylophobia raged inside her, and she swayed, like a fir top-heavy with snow. She reached out, steadying herself against Corineus. *Don't have a seizure.*

She looked again. Her mom looked so different. Weary. Older. So much older. Older even than Grandma Ivy. How? Why? And why was she just sitting there?

Genza shot a glance at Bibi and Corineus—Bibi understood he meant them to be quiet until he could figure out what was happening.

Over by the two-trunked tree, Alenka the lioness spoke— addressing Nan Blundermuss in a voice that seemed to slither across the ground.

"Tell us who you are, stranger," she said.

Nan looked up. Bibi saw then that she held a dead Falanthrow flower in one hand—tenderly, as if it were an injured bird—and a branch in the other.

The branch from the photo! The Arbor Guardian's branch. At last, it made sense. A *wand*.

The hylophobia worsened as Bibi watched—the pain like worms burrowing through her stomach. The ground beneath her seemed to rock back and forth, like the deck of a sea-tossed ship. She began to have the feeling of shrinking into nothingness—was that the seizure at last?

Concentrate on something else. She watched her mom's shoulders going up and down with her breath. *Inhale, exhale.*

Instead of answering Alenka, Nan began waving her branch over the flower. Bibi's heart raced—was she going to do the Quickening? Please do the Quickening!

"Enough, Alenka," Gorka said. "Let's kill her and find Lord Valmyr and the others."

No! Bibi bit her lip. But Alenka just watched as Nan closed her eyes, passing the branch over the flower again.

"*Khula*," Nan said, her voice quiet, but strong as a root ball.

Even from a distance, Bibi saw a burst of crimson come to the flower's petals, like a cloud of blood entering a pool. The color spread to the edges, taking on a red-orange tint—and the flower's petals stiffened, forming a star shape as large as a dinner plate. Nan cupped it with both hands, as a bit of glittery pollen spilled out, accompanied by the wind chime sound.

Bibi stifled a yelp. She had already accepted that her mom was a witch—but to see the magic, before her eyes! It was incredible. Ellery Finley would not have believed it.

Nan sighed heavily, as if exhausted by her effort.

The lions retched when the scent of the revived flower's pollen reached them. They stepped back, exposing their teeth. From a safer distance, Alenka snarled, sweeping her tail across the dirt.

"What sorcery is this?" she said. "Are you a demon?"

Nan seemed to get a second wind. She rose to her feet, lifting the revived flower over her head, as if offering it to the Cosmos. With a white-hot glare, she seethed at the lions. "No, Trolliclawian," she said, her voice growing distorted and deep. "I am not a demon. I am an Arbor Guardian!" She drew her other arm back, and swept the branch in front of her, in a broad, fluid motion. "*KHULA!*"

The ground quaked, and hot energy radiated from Nan's branch in all directions. It passed under Bibi and Corineus and Genza, and into the surrounding trees. The Falanthrows flashed, as if consumed by explosive fire—so bright that Bibi had to cover her eyes.

When the flash abated, a lazy warmth crept over Splitwood. Bibi opened her eyes and lifted her head. She seemed to have fallen into a summer day. The nearby Harrowing mist had burned away—though Bibi could still see it in the distance. This part of the forest now teemed with living trees, abundant with red-orange star-shaped flowers that quavered in a balmy breeze blown in from nowhere. The sparkling pollen rained down from their branches like showers of sunlight, immersing the air with the gingery smell and the sound of wind chimes.

The Quickening! It must be the Quickening! At last! For a second, Bibi stood in awe of her mom's power, until more dizziness hit her—like a sudden wind—and her stomach felt squeezed again, as if pinched with pliers. She was still among the trees. The shrinking feeling came back—surely the seizure would follow.

Even in her pain, Bibi heard a quiet, grating, desperate sound. She turned. The lions, surrounded by living trees and flowers, were suffering too. *Pollen from the Falanthrow trees is deadly to the Trolliclawians*, Corineus had said. Alenka and Gorka quickly succumbed to Falanthrow poisoning, falling to the ground before Nan, tongues lolling and sides heaving. Fighting for breath, they foamed at the mouth, staring with reddened eyes.

"Curse you, Arbor Guardian," Alenka spat, writhing and gagging. "Demon! *Curse you.*"

Nan pulled her branch and flower back to her chest.

"Listen carefully," she said. "I could kill you. But I need your help."

Bibi was uncertain she had heard that right. Her ears rang, sound distorted by hylophobia. Her mouth felt dry, her skin clammy. Their *help*? Had her mom asked for the Trolliclawians' *help*? Zezo thought she had joined the white lions, but surely Zezo had been wrong. Right? *Stay focused.*

Nan breathed deep and made the swiping motion with her branch again. She erased the vibrant scene as easily as brushing hoof prints from riverbank sand. Death returned: the white mist blew back in, and the trees hardened until they were once more black and stony, their leaves and flowers evaporating into dust that drifted to the hard forest floor, as the pollen had done moments before. Only Nan's flower remained alive. It gave off a lonely red-orange radiance, protecting her.

Bibi could not believe it. Why would her mom stop the Quickening like that?

The two lions did not seem to believe it either. Recovering from the exposure, they crawled back to sit, facing Nan at a careful distance. They showed their teeth again, with a mixture of rage and respect.

"What do you *want*, Arbor Guardian?" Alenka said, after a pause.

Nan stood taller, her voice scornful. "You have no idea what you are involved in. It is much bigger than you—much bigger than Trolliclawians and elk." She set her jaw. "Take me to your king. The lion called Valmyr. I have a proposal for him."

Bibi glanced at Corineus and Genza. Genza's injuries suddenly looked worse, magnified by the shock on his face.

Alenka straightened her tail, but otherwise did not react.

"*No*, Alenka," Gorka warned.

Alenka bared her teeth at him, then turned back to Nan. "And if our king, the mighty Lord Valmyr, will not see you?" she said, finally.

Nan lowered her head, and a shadow fell across her face.

"Then I will restore the forest and lay waste to all the lions."

Bibi could hardly think straight. If her mom could invoke the Quickening at will, was she *allowing* the Harrowing to kill

128

the trees? Why wouldn't she make the Quickening last? Why wouldn't she make it spread through Falanthrow Forest, and drive the white lions away for good? Shouldn't the Arbor Guardian do that?

Had Zezo been right?

Finally, Alenka inclined her head, and she and Gorka rose to their feet. "Very well," the lioness said. "This way."

They turned to slink off into the mist—Gorka grumbling his assent. Before following, Nan waited long enough to peer behind her—in the direction of Bibi, Corineus, and Genza, who still had not moved, just a few hundred feet away. Couldn't she see them? Bibi's hands trembled—she wanted to call out, but felt weak, powerless. She had come all this way. *Mom is right there.*

Something—the hylophobia, the lions, the look on Genza's face, or a new and terrifying uncertainty about the woman in front of her—kept Bibi still and silent. If Nan did see her, she gave no indication, but instead turned away again, following the lions into the dead forest.

CHAPTER THIRTY-TWO:
Fallout

When Nan had gone with the lions, Genza, though still haggard and bloody, spun to face Bibi. Rage burned like a forest fire in his eyes.

"The Arbor Guardian betrayed us!" he said.

"No!" Corineus said, stepping in front of the older elk. "Genza, listen—"

"Zezo was right!" Genza said. "The Arbor Guardian joined the Trolliclawians! Sweet Yega-Woo is lost!" He was inconsolable.

No! Bibi grew numb, with the blood seeming to drain from her body, and her body seeming to shrink away. The dead trees, all around them. The clenching in her gut became uncontrollable, and she dropped to her knees, vomiting violently.

"Bibi Blundermuss!" Corineus said, turning desperately from

Genza, lowering his head next to her, his voice barely audible over the ringing in her ears. "Please hold on!"

Wiping her mouth, Bibi thought of the day she had come to this strange world. *This will not make sense at first,* her mom had said. *Our lives depend on you.* Well, it didn't make sense at first, and it didn't make sense now. And her mom had it backwards. Bibi's life—and Eek's, and the elk's—everyone's lives depended on *her.* Why wouldn't she make the Quickening last? Why had she . . . betrayed them?

NO! Bibi struggled to rise to her feet—but couldn't. Something held her body in a twisted knot. Something—a seizure! She saw Corineus and Genza both speaking to her—compassion in Corineus's face, fury in Genza's. But the high-pitched ringing in her ears made it impossible to understand them. Only some words got through.

"Please hold on!"

"Your mother betrayed us!"

"Careful, careful, careful!"

Bibi felt tiny and helpless—like a leaf on the surface of cold River Eldred.

A question flitted through her mind as she grappled to stay awake and aware—did Praetor Wight, or Anaspiritus, have something to do with her mom going off with the lions? She couldn't think clearly. The ringing got louder, like someone banging a heavy bell against her skull. She felt for the photo in her pants pocket. At least she still had it. Soggy and torn, but she still had it.

Corineus looked at her wildly. He appeared to be shouting.

131

I can't understand you. Bibi felt her lips forming the words, but it was like trying to speak through a mouth full of peanut butter.

She saw he wanted her to get on his back. Yes. With the last of her strength she climbed up—but even clinging to him, like clinging to a rock in the rapids, she seemed to be somersaulting through the air, while her jaw and tongue hung heavy.

I thought Mom was a good person. I thought she could fix this.

The hylophobia surged, like an enormous, murderous wisteria, wrapping around her and squeezing until she could hardly breathe. The forest spun—a dark, haunted merry-go-round.

Bibi went comatose.

PART THREE
THE QUICKENING

CHAPTER THIRTY-THREE:
After the Dead Forest

A bracing gasp. Like the first breath of a newborn.

Inhale. Exhale.

So cold. Bibi's body ached with the throb of a fading flu. She was on her back, on hard ground—the sky open above her, a cloudless blue. There were no trees.

No trees? How could that be?

Where was she? How had she gotten here? She dug through the debris of her memory—like fallen branches after a storm. Eek. Lions. Elk. Falanthrow Forest. She sat up, trying to focus.

Mom. What had happened?

She shivered. It felt like weeks had gone by.

She saw a rocky slope rising before her, scattered with scree, in black and gray and silver. Not far away, it steepened into looming cliffs and peaks. She thought back to the day she arrived in Falanthrow Forest, and the black mountains surrounding it. Corineus had called them the Black Crest Mountains. Was that where she was?

No trees. *No trees.*

Slowly Bibi rose to her feet, knees wobbly. She looked around, hugging her denim jacket against the chill, her breath visible in the air. It had been warm in the clearing, and cool in the forest—but here it was quite chilly, like the first day of winter. It seemed to be morning—the sun somewhere behind the mountains but rising.

She didn't want to be alone. She had a faint memory of being with Corineus and Genza—where were they?

"Hello?" she said, her voice tasting dry as dead grass.

As if in answer, clopping hooves sounded among the rocks. Bibi turned to see Corineus coming up a path by one of the nearby boulders. Instantly, her shoulders relaxed. *Not alone.*

He looked different somehow. Still little, but taller and thinner. His tuft of hair thicker. Had that much time passed? Seeing her, he hurried over. "Bibi Blundermuss," he said, anxiously. "You're awake!"

Before Bibi could respond, the strength drained from her legs. She found a flat rock and sat, taking another deep breath. She rubbed her temples with her thumbs.

"Oh, Cori," she said. "What happened? How did we get here?"

"You've been asleep," Corineus said, moving closer, brushing his wet nose against her, as if making sure she was really okay. "For a long time."

Bibi paused. Asleep? She didn't feel rested at all. She felt exhausted.

"How long?"

Corineus shrugged. "A *long* time. More than a full black moon."

A full black moon. Was that a month? Bibi slumped. It didn't matter. Time had passed. That's why he looked different—he had grown. And she . . . of course. The seizure, and then . . . she had gone comatose. Like the book had predicted. The hylophobia had won.

"And you stayed with me?" Bibi said, as her tears brimmed.

"Of course."

Bibi felt something twist in her, like someone tying a knot there. Not the hylophobia—the memory, returning. How they met the white lions in the forest. How Yega-Woo lured Valmyr away. Her mom's . . . betrayal? That's what Genza thought, right? In her mind, she still saw his angry look.

A bitter taste came to her tongue. She had thought that, too. How could she have thought that? *Mom is a good person. Mom is a good person.* She gently beat her forehead with the heel of a fist.

"The bees helped us," Corineus said, interrupting her thoughts.

Bibi sat up straight. The bees! The ones who had summoned her in the first place. "I thought Valmyr killed them?"

Corineus shook his head. "There are more bees here than you met that first day. They are Arbor Guardian bees, and have some magic, too. When I got you out of the forest, they gave you the honey that kept you alive."

Bibi frowned. Could she really have survived on bee honey for a month, while comatose? Well, if they were her mom's bees, maybe.

She sighed. How could her mom have gotten so old? And why, why, why hadn't Bibi called out to her that day in the forest? Wouldn't that have fixed everything? How could she have been so stupid?

"At first, Genza and I tried to take you back to the clearing, but the trees around it had died," Corineus said. "Then the Alala came. The warrior elk—like the old ones told us."

"The Alala?" Bibi placed her arms over her belly. She was beginning to realize how hungry she was. Magic honey was one thing, but she needed *food.*

"Hundreds of them," Corineus said. "Huge stags with sharp antlers. Strong does with powerful kicking legs. They knew nothing of the Arbor Guardian." He looked down. "They only wanted war with the Trolliclawians."

Bibi widened her eyes. "Did you tell them what happened to us? How we barely escaped?"

Corineus smiled, nodding. "The thing is . . . after that day, the white lions went away. We haven't seen them since." He faced her. "There is a place called the Tunnel Rocks—a labyrinth of caves to the west, in the foothills of the Black Crest Mountains. The Alala say the Trolliclawians are hiding there. They plan to attack soon. They say the lions are afraid."

That sounded impossible. "Afraid of what?"

"Of the Alala." A sad look passed into Corineus's eyes—like a cloud of sediment kicked up from a river bed. "And Genza has joined the Alala. He's become a warrior. A full woodskull. A hard life—always running. He's gone mad, Bibi Blundermuss. You wouldn't recognize him. It's because of Yega-Woo. After Valmyr, she never came back. Genza loved her, you know." He choked back a sob.

Yega-Woo never came back? It was too much. Bibi sat cross-legged, with her elbows on her knees, and her chin on her palms, fighting the tears. Her stomach growled—not with hylophobia, but with aching hunger. What should they do? She wished Yega-Woo was still here. She wished Aruna, and even Baranji and Zezo were still here. She did not want Genza to be with the Alala, and she did not want to be anywhere near a battle between lions and warrior elk. She wanted to find Eek— probably still with the lions, too. And most of all, she wanted to find her mom, who had gone to be with Lord Valmyr, King of the Trolliclawians—but not, Bibi decided, to betray her friends. There had to be some other reason. There *had* to be.

Bibi stood up—and this time she remained upright. She had to get her strength back somehow. She walked over to Corineus and gently ran a hand along his spine.

"Cori," she said. "Which way to the Tunnel Rocks?"

Hesitantly, Corineus pointed with his nose.

"I have to go there," she said. "There's something I'm missing. Mom is a good person."

The little elk looked at the ground. "I'll go, too. Yega-Woo would want us to find her."

Bibi leaned down, so she could look him in the eyes. "I'm so sorry about Yega-Woo, Cori." She tried her best to sound confident. "But Mom will fix this. She'll fix everything, I promise. She's the Arbor Guardian, remember?" She set her jaw, and stood straight again, rubbing her stomach. "Now, before we go—can we find something to eat?"

CHAPTER THIRTY-FOUR:
The Circle Road

Corineus took Bibi to a cache of nuts and berries he had stored in a nearby cave. Once they got their fill, they began walking down the slope—Corineus stepping carefully among the hard rocks. As they got lower, Bibi saw Falanthrow Forest in the distance—maybe a five-minute walk from where they were. Scarves of mist lingered in the trees' blackened branches. She suppressed a small tremor of worry.

Soon they reached a dirt road—narrow and worn, skirting the edge of the forest in both directions. Corineus stopped.

"The Tunnel Rocks are on the other side of the forest," he said, looking along the road. "Climb on. The Circle Road will lead us there. We can avoid the trees." He gave her a searching look.

Bibi's face flushed. She stole another glance at Falanthrow

Forest—now close enough to make her queasy. She pulled herself onto his back, relieved for a different way to go.

All morning Corineus galloped along the Circle Road, kicking up a cloud of dust. Bibi held on tight. They did not speak much. The day did not get warmer—and aside from the low scrub that grew in pockets of pale green among the mountain rubble, there was nothing to see but dirt and rocks.

But the rocks were not all the same. Once, Bibi noticed a mound of them—a little bigger than an elk, oddly piled on the side of the road, with bits of bone and plant remains mixed in.

"What was that?" she said after they passed it.

"It's called a midden," Corineus said. "The lions made them, long ago—trash heaps that marked the edge of their mountain kingdom, as reminders to not go into the forest. Back in the days when the trees could kill them."

"Are there more middens?"

"All around the Circle Road. One will come up again soon enough."

Bibi rubbed her nose as they rushed through the cold air. She spotted snow, high up on the Black Crest Mountains. She pictured the Trolliclawians living up there in the snowy peaks, before the Harrowing. And then, as predicted: another midden. And soon: another, and another, spaced at a regular distance. One every mile, maybe? Counting them helped break up the monotony and kept her mind off the black forest to their right.

Ten . . . eleven . . . twelve . . .

By the thirteenth midden, the sun reached the center of the sky. There, it shone down with diffused warmth. In the mid-day brightness, Corineus began looking more frequently from side to side. Eventually, he slowed.

"Are we close?" Bibi said.

The little elk looked at her encouragingly but said nothing. He stepped with caution, ready to sprint again if needed. Bibi's heart banged like a brass door knocker against her chest. She could hardly bear the anticipation. If they were close to where the lions were hidden, Eek might be here! Mom might be here!

At last, Corineus stopped completely. Though the landscape appeared deserted, Bibi felt that someone was watching them. With shaking legs, the little elk moved off the road, taking cover behind one of the middens.

"What is it?" Bibi said.

Corineus still did not answer but waited unmoving in the shadow of the heap. Bibi's legs felt sore from the ride, so she slid off his back and onto the ground, as quietly as she could. She stared at the bleached bones mingled with the ancient rock pile.

"Did you hear it?" Corineus whispered, turning to her. "A scratching sound?"

Bibi strained her ears. She could only hear a light wind blowing across the Circle Road. "No. Are we there?"

"The Tunnel Rocks are hard to see from the outside," Corineus said, under his breath. "Maybe we passed them by mistake."

"You did not pass them," said a voice.

143

Bibi knew that voice well. She turned and almost fainted with joy.

Perched on top of the midden, Eek looked down at them.

CHAPTER THIRTY-FIVE:
The Mysterious Eek

Eek—after all this time! Bibi could hardly think what to say, so she said the first thing that came to mind: "*Sawubona,* Eek!"

She waited. The little black cat, silhouetted by the cold noon sun, did not move or speak.

The top of the midden was too high for Bibi to reach. How come Eek just sat there? Why didn't she respond? She seemed so . . . stoic. She resembled an Egyptian figurine Bibi had seen at the Natural History Museum—utterly still, except for her tail, which peeked teasingly over the edge of the highest rock.

Finally, Eek bowed her head. "That's her," she said, her voice almost inaudible. She shifted her green eyes to the left.

Bibi turned to follow her cat's gaze, and her heart sank. No, no, no!

Alenka and Gorka. The lions who had been with Valmyr

at the River Eldred. The lions who had gone off with her mom. They stood next to the midden, staring at Bibi with eyes hard and inscrutable, like cut glass.

Bibi dug her fingernails into her palms, trying not to panic. She tried to speak, but the words sat like dirt on her tongue. She felt Corineus trembling next to her.

"Daughter of Nan Blundermuss," Alenka said. Bibi's mom's name sounded wrong in the lioness's mouth. Gorka took a step closer, and another—only stopping when his face was a few inches from Bibi's, with his breath of metal and bile.

"Come with us," he said. "Or we kill the runt elk."

Clutching her stomach, Bibi turned to Corineus, remembering the blood stripes Valmyr had painted on his haunches—faded under the fur in the weeks since. Corineus's teeth were chattering audibly. Bibi looked at Eek again—but Eek remained still. This didn't make sense.

"G-g-go away," Corineus finally said to the lions. "Leave us alone."

Gorka gave him a withering look, and he shrank back. "Not exactly a woodskull yet, are you, boy?" Gorka said. "What are you going to do—shake your hair at us?"

"Eek, what's going on?" Bibi said to her little black cat, suddenly furious. "Is this any way to treat a friend?"

Still sitting at the top of the midden, Eek said nothing, avoiding Bibi's gaze.

Alenka glowered at Eek. "You told Lord Valmyr you could find the daughter of Nan Blundermuss, black catling. You didn't say you were friends. *Are* you friends?"

Bibi stared at her cat.

"No," Eek said, her voice flat. She rose to make her way down the pile of rocks, as nonchalantly as if she was moving from the food bowl to the couch.

No? Bibi's anger burned brighter as she reached a finger behind her glasses to wipe away a hot tear. Now she had to worry about *Eek's* betrayal? Why? What to believe? Who to trust? She thought of how the Ash tree brought them here all those days ago, turning everything upside-down.

She paused.

For a split second, as Eek neared the bottom of the midden, something glinted in her green eyes. Bibi glanced at the lions. Neither had seen it. Bibi wondered if *she* had really seen it. It seemed some kind of secret message—like a signal in a fog.

Corineus, body shaking all over, said, "What do you want, Trolliclawians?"

Gorka narrowed his eyes sharply. "The king of the white lions wants you, little no-woodskull, to go tell the Alala to attack." He looked at Bibi. "And he wants you, daughter of Nan Blundermuss, to come with us. We're going to pay a visit to your mother."

Mom!

Fingertips tingling, Bibi watched Eek arrive at the bottom of the midden. Tail undulating, the little black cat stepped delicately through the dust until she reached the Trolliclawians. Bibi wrangled with her fury and despair and excitement. Something didn't make sense here. *Think!*

147

"It's a trap, Bibi Blundermuss," Corineus said, looking at her with growing alarm. His voice shook so much he could hardly get the words out.

Alenka snarled. "Enough, runt elk. Go back to the Alala while you still can. Tell them to attack."

Corineus closed his eyes, shaking his head. "It's a trap, it's a trap, it's a trap . . ."

Bibi looked from Eek to the lions. Maybe it *was* a trap. But for who? Eek may have been smaller than Alenka and Gorka, but she was much cleverer.

The glint in her green eyes. That must be it.

"I'll go," Bibi said, before she could change her mind. "It's okay, Cori. I've got this."

Corineus, still shaking, looked so surprised that for a moment she feared he might crumble away into a pile of dust and bones, to be added to the midden. A grin spread across Gorka's face, like a noxious fissure opening in the ground.

Alenka sighed. "Come on, then." Bibi tried to ignore her thudding heart. Eek must want this. She must have some secret plan. And if these lions could take her to her mom . . .

She hugged Corineus around the neck, hoping he would understand, and trying to get him to stop shaking. His fur was cold. She whispered: "Tell the Alala to wait. I'll get Mom to heal the forest, I promise. I'll see you again, I just know it!"

"Okay," he said—but she wasn't sure he believed her. She set her jaw and joined her little black cat and the Trolliclawians as they moved past the midden heap, across the Circle Road, and toward the slope of the mountain—marching into the unknown. All because of a secret message, flashing in her cat's green eyes.

When she turned to wave to Corineus, her friend was gone.

CHAPTER THIRTY-SIX:
Something Sweet in the Air

After a few minutes' climb, Alenka pointed to a canyon that ran parallel to the Circle Road. They entered. The walls cut so deep that Bibi could no longer see up or down the slope. The sky went by in a sliver of cold blue above them.

Eek trotted ahead, lifting her paws high, as if nothing was wrong. Bibi followed, with the lions behind—so close that she could feel their hot breath on her back. She refused to look at them. She tried to keep from shaking. Either of them could have killed her with one swipe of a paw—but they hadn't. That meant they wanted her alive.

Out in front, Eek playfully hunted a hovering fly. Bibi slowed to watch, though she had seen her cat do this thousands of times. It didn't make sense—this was no time for games! Eek lowered her belly to the ground, and crawled toward the insect, paw over paw. She pounced and missed, and then began the hunt anew.

"Keep moving," Gorka said.

Picking up her pace again, Bibi took a deep breath, and, without turning to face the white lions, spoke as forcefully as she could, trying not to allow fear into her voice.

"I'm not scared of you. My mom will protect me."

No response—nothing but the dull steady *thud thud thud* of paws in the dirt.

Bibi stood straighter, emboldened. She had lied—she certainly was scared. But she wanted to keep the lions talking—to push them. Maybe they would reveal something that would give her a clue to Eek's plan. She thought back to that day at the river. "Valmyr didn't kill Genza, you know. He didn't finish the job. Genza joined the Alala."

She could feel Alenka's annoyance.

"Quiet, daughter of Nan Blundermuss."

Eek gave Bibi a sidelong glance—another green-eyed glint—and went back to stalking the fly, further ahead. What did it mean? Bibi worried she might be imagining things. Her fingertips tingled again. No. *Something is happening—think.*

When Alenka spoke again, her voice rose like steam from a vent. "Everything is about to change, daughter of Nan Blundermuss. When your mother sees you, we Trolliclawians will finally be able to go back into Falanthrow Forest. And that will be the end of the elk."

Her voice trailed off. Bibi wished she could read the lioness's expression, but she still wouldn't turn around, fearful of the sight.

151

They walked on. Ahead, other flies joined the first, and Eek continued stalking.

"I don't know what you're talking about," Bibi said. "My mom is the Arbor Guardian. She is very powerful. You can't beat her." She reached into her pocket to make sure the photograph of her parents was still there.

Gorka growled, lacing the canyon air with his sharp metallic scent. "Maybe *we* can't," he said. "But King Valmyr can, with the right *hostage.*"

The word hit Bibi like a punch. But before she could reply, Eek sprinted closer, her tail bowed down like a rudder, a small cloud of dust in her wake. She zig-zagged between the canyon walls, followed by a growing buzz—the flies she had been chasing now chased her.

Bibi adjusted her glasses with a forefinger. Those weren't flies! There was a hint of something sweet in the air. A hint of . . .

Honey. *Honey!*

They were bees.

Her mom's bees!

There were many more bees than had lured Bibi to the sapling on that day back home. As if cued, huge billowing black plumes of them poured out of the walls on either side of the canyon. The rocks vibrated with their buzzing. The swarm spread overhead, between the canyon walls—a giant bee blanket thrown across the sky, turning day into night.

Something brushed by Bibi's leg. *Eek!* The little black cat looked up at her, green eyes brighter, whiskers peeled back.

"Bibi!" Eek said, her voice almost drowned out by the

sound of the insects. "This way!" She dashed off to the side without waiting.

Bibi turned to the lions, who stared at the bee-pall with frothing rage, their great tails lashing like prehistoric serpents.

"What foolishness is this!"

"Black catling!"

"Bibi!" Eek cried again, from the side of the canyon.

Bibi tore herself from her stupor—scrambling out of the way, over to where her cat was.

"Bees—*now!*" Eek shouted to the sky.

At her words, the terrible bee-cloud roared down upon Gorka and Alenka, like an endless volley of tiny poison darts, covering them until they could no longer be seen.

CHAPTER THIRTY-SEVEN:
The Tunnel Rocks

Moving away from the bees, Bibi ran hard, a few steps behind Eek. She pressed her hands to her ears, trying to shut out the thunderous noise of the attacking swarm. But she could still hear the lions' horrible shrieks beneath it all.

Soon, Eek slipped into a crack in the canyon wall. "Come on!" she said, vanishing into the darkness. Bibi forced herself through too.

The cave was dim and dusty—too shallow to stand up in, and sparsely illuminated by light from the canyon. "Where are you, Eek?" Bibi said. She could hardly hear her own voice over the bee buzzing that echoed against the stone walls.

"This way!" came the reply. Ahead, Eek's silhouette moved deeper into the cave. Bibi scrambled forward.

The rocky, uneven ground tore at her knees. She scraped

a palm on a jagged rock, leaving a dab of blood. When they got a little farther in, the bee buzz dwindled to a hum. Clumps of *Photinus foliosa*, the phosphorescent plant Bibi had seen on High Hill, grew against the walls, making it light enough to see.

"Where are you, Eek?" Bibi said again.

"*Sawubona,* Bibi!" Eek said, stepping out of the shadows.

At last. Bibi embraced her, and they laughed, despite welling tears. The cat purred, nudging Bibi's chin, warm and soft against her, eyes closed and nose joyfully pointed to the tunnel ceiling.

"*Sawubona,* Eek," Bibi said, smiling so hard that it hurt. Words and feelings came gushing like a fountain. "I was so worried. I *knew* you couldn't be friends with the lions. I'm so happy to see you. What happened? How did you get here? Where's Mom? She'll fix everything, if I can just find her!"

Water ran in a noisy trickle down the wall, pooling at the bottom, and disappearing through a narrow channel. "Hold on," Eek said, squirming out of Bibi's arms and crouching to drink, with little slurping noises. Bibi, thirsty too, scooped some of the water into her mouth with cupped hands. It was freezing cold and stung the scrape on her palm. She wiped her hands on her jeans.

Eek stopped drinking, and, licking her lips, sat back. She yawned an enormous yawn, showing off her small white teeth.

"I have so much to tell you, Bibi. But we have to keep moving. I'll explain as we go."

"Okay," Bibi said, and they continued deeper into the cave.

CHAPTER THIRTY-EIGHT:
What Happened to Nan

"After the white lions found me," Eek said, her small voice echoing against the big rocks as she padded along, "they thought I was one of theirs. They called me black catling. I guess the lions only turn white when they become grownups."

Bibi nodded. "We saw you go."

"*Mrow.* We? Who?"

"Corineus and me."

"The little elk with the funny hairdo and sad eyes?"

Bibi nodded again. "Don't make fun of him! I wouldn't be here if not for him." A current of colder air passed by from somewhere deeper in the cave. She shivered as she crawled on.

"Sorry," Eek said. "Anyway, the lions made me come with them here, to the Tunnel Rocks. I had to pretend I belonged. I had been with them a few days, trying to figure out an escape, when your mom showed up!"

Bibi was so excited that she bumped her head on a low-hanging bulge of stone. "Is she with Valmyr, the king of the white lions?"

Eek rubbed the side of her face against an outcrop, as if it was the corner of the dining room chair. "Yes—how did you know that?" she said, tail upright like a sunflower stalk. "She's in his cave. She won't leave his side."

The flame of hope that had been rekindling in Bibi's chest began to flicker. Her mom wouldn't leave Valmyr's side? It didn't make sense. She crawled faster, trying to keep up.

"Never mind how I know about Valmyr—why is she with the lions at all? Why isn't she helping the elk? Isn't that what she came here to do? Is Dad with her? What's a *Praetor Wight*? And—"

Eek protested the deluge of questions with a loud whine. They reached a place where the tunnel got taller. Bibi stood, pursing her lips, waiting for Eek's answer, and they walked on in silence for a time.

"Do you know your mom is a witch?" Eek said at last. She spoke as if still getting used to the idea herself.

"*Arbor Guardian*," Bibi said, impatiently. "I know. She can bring dead trees back to life. I saw her do it!"

Eek stopped, curling and uncurling her tail.

"And do you remember how she said she needs your help?"

Bibi paused. "Yes," she said. She thought back to her mom's message—the one the bees brought. *Our lives depend on you.* But how could that be true?

157

Bibi waited while Eek cleaned her whiskers in the yellow-green light. She thought she heard strange noises ahead. Before she could ask what they were, Eek urged them forward again.

"The white lions think your mom can grow Falanthrow trees wherever she wants—in the forest, along the Circle Road, even on the mountain," Eek said. "They are afraid of her."

"Well, they *should* be!" Bibi said. "But that doesn't explain why she is with them."

Eek purred. "Bibi, she tricked them. The Trolliclawians are very loyal to Valmyr. And when they took her to him, she took him hostage. That's how she protects the elk—the lions know not to harm the elk, or she will kill Valmyr."

Bibi felt a little lighter. "I *knew* she wasn't on the lions' side!" She hesitated, folding her arms. "But wait—that still doesn't make sense! Why did she have to take King Valmyr hostage? She's the Arbor Guardian!"

Eek meowed, then dropped her voice. "Because she *can't* grow Falanthrow trees wherever she wants. Not anymore. She can't even grow Falanthrow trees in Falanthrow Forest. She has changed. The lions don't know it, but her power has been getting weaker ever since she came here. All she can do is keep a few Falanthrow flowers alive in Valmyr's cave—enough to keep him hostage."

No. Bibi shook her head. That couldn't be true.

She heard the strange noise again. It sounded like more lions. It was hard to tell what they were doing—Bibi heard muffled shrieks and skittering claws.

"She's losing her power," Eek said, ignoring the sound. "And the lions are beginning to suspect something. She needs your help, before they figure it out. That's why she sent the bees to find us. And that's why she sent me to find you."

Mom . . . losing her power? No, there must be some other explanation. Something Eek hadn't understood. Bibi wrinkled her nose. The foul metallic odor was back. They were definitely getting close to the white lions.

"So, Mom sent you to find me—and Valmyr did, too?"

"I told him I could find you, and he sent the three of us— me, Gorka, Alenka. He did not know that your mom wanted me to find you anyway." Eek's voice had lowered to a whisper.

"So, you led the lions right to me?"

"What choice did I have? If I didn't, I couldn't protect you." The little black cat lifted her head high. "I knew the bees would help. They were the ones who told me where you were. And they'd been looking to get their revenge on the lions since the day we arrived in Falanthrow Forest."

Bibi rubbed her chin, thinking. Trying to keep track of everything made her head go around. What had her mom said to Alenka? *This is much bigger than you.* Very true!

Ahead, new light came into the cave, from an opening in the wall—a few feet wide, and hip-height from the ground. Eek leapt up to it.

"This goes to another tunnel," she said, in a hush. "And that goes to the cave where your mother is." She paused, listening to the lion sounds as they grew louder. "There are Trolliclawians on the other side. We will have to get to the cave without them seeing us. Are you ready?"

159

Bibi couldn't believe they were so close. Her heart thrummed against her ribcage, like a rabbit stamping its feet.

No. Not like a rabbit. Rabbits were timid. She needed to be brave. Could she be brave?

"Let's go," she said.

CHAPTER THIRTY-NINE:
Deepening Shadows

Following Eek, Bibi crawled into the opening, and found herself in a shaft about twice as long as she was. She moved forward on her abdomen, trying not to catch her denim jacket on the rocks overhead, and listening to the lion sounds from the other side. When they reached the end, Eek went through, and Bibi carefully stuck her head out.

The shaft opened into another tunnel, as Eek had described. It was bigger around than the first. Light and the lion sounds came from the left, where the tunnel led to an open-air stone atrium, perhaps fifty yards away. Bibi could see several white lions there, darting around in front of the opening.

"Get him!" one of them growled to his comrades.

"Draw blood!" said another.

They were fighting each other—but why?

Meanwhile, Eek crouched on the ground in front of Bibi, down where it was dark.

"Bibi!" she whispered. "Climb out!"

In the atrium, one of the Trolliclawians scrambled over to the tunnel opening. He sat facing out, blocking much of the light with his muscular body. After taking a moment to catch his breath, he laughed.

"Don't be shy, boys," he said. "Claws out!"

From the hole in the wall, Bibi pulled her bottom half into the tunnel, as smoothly as she could. When nearly all the way out, she slipped, tumbling down to the tunnel floor with a shower of pebbles and dust.

She darted another glance toward the atrium. The sitting Trolliclawian hadn't heard or moved—he remained preoccupied with whatever was going on in the open space.

"Come on!" Eek whispered, pattering the other way.

The tunnel was more than big enough for Bibi to stand. She scrambled to her feet and followed her cat. With every step, the shadows deepened. She reached out to touch the wall, steadying herself.

"Eek, slow down!" she said. "I can't see!" Was Valmyr near?

A muted shriek came from the atrium. Bibi spun around. She saw that the tunnel opening had emptied—but she could still hear the lions nearby.

"Very well," one of them said, after a pause, and in a more subdued tone. "It's his turn today. Dig in, boys. But be sure to save some for Lord Valmyr."

After his words came other sounds—lacerating and wet.

Bibi shuddered. She couldn't let herself think about what they were doing. Eek wove around her legs, urging her deeper into the tunnel. Bibi turned and followed the path as it curved, until the light from the atrium faded.

"There!" Eek said at last.

Unable to see, Bibi sensed something in front of her and stopped. She reached out to touch a flat surface—a screen, woven from reeds and grass and sticks, propped against a rock that protruded from the ceiling.

Ready to run if need be, she carefully lifted the screen and moved it aside.

Colored light spilled into the tunnel. Ahead grew an abundance of yellow-green *Photinus foliosa*. But there were blotches of red-orange too, scattered across the floor like little magma chambers. They caught the *Photinus* light, reflecting it back and giving the cave a harsh glow.

Falanthrow flowers. They reeked with a heavy ginger-honey scent—so sweet in the enclosed space that it burned the back of Bibi's throat.

"Mom?" she whispered, as the cave came into focus.

Eek, wobbling on her feet a little, wheezed as if to produce a hairball. Bibi realized the flowers affected her like they affected the Trolliclawians. "Are you okay, Eek?" she asked.

"Your mom gave me a cat-grass antidote. I'll be better in a minute. *Mrow*—look!"

"Where? Is she here? I don't see her." Bibi trembled, as the details of the cave became clearer, revealing a ghost-white shape on the ground.

She blenched.

Valmyr. He looked so much bigger in the small cave. He lay on his side, either asleep or unconscious. A layer of white film covered his open eyes. He gulped for breath through his red dagger-size fangs.

He must have been badly poisoned by the flowers. Still, she couldn't relax—she remembered the chase by the River Eldred. She assumed the huge lion might rise and lunge at her, zombie-like, at any moment.

Her voice was a wisp as she turned to Eek. "Where's Mom!"

There was another shape, sitting farther back in the gloom, perhaps twenty feet behind Valmyr.

The shape stirred, and Bibi bit back a cry. The grimy cloak. The weary, sunken eyes. The slate-gray braids. The skin ashy and worn.

"Mom!"

CHAPTER FORTY:
The King of the White Lions

Nan Blundermuss looked positively ancient, but somewhere under the layers of dust and worry and exhaustion burned the ember of her warm smile.

"Hello, Acorn," she said, in a quiet, shaky voice. "I was beginning to wonder if you'd ever come."

Without a word, recklessly, Bibi ran across the carpet of Falanthrow flowers, past the ghastly, prostrate Valmyr, until she reached her mom. Collapsing, she laid her head in the strangely aged woman's lap, sobbing.

Eek followed, sitting next to them, but turning to keep an eye on the Trolliclawian king.

"There, there, Acorn," Nan said, stroking Bibi's hair, like when she was small. "We're together again! Didn't I tell you? Everything is going to be okay."

Bibi could not believe the frailty of her mother's hand. She could feel the bones in each finger. The dark skin, dotted with age spots, hung looser than she remembered.

"Mom—what happened to you?" she said, unable to stop staring.

Nan studied the rock floor. "It's the fate of an Arbor Guardian working alone," she said. "After six months, even keeping these Falanthrow flowers alive is taxing." She drew her lips together. "Let's begin." She reached into her cloak and produced a branch.

Bibi stared. The same branch her mom had used to bring the trees back to life, back in the forest. The same branch she held for the photo in Bibi's pocket. She pointed it toward Bibi.

"Begin what?" Bibi said.

"Hush, Acorn! Let me concentrate." Nan inhaled and closed her eyes. Her face became stony. With great solemnity, she spoke a single word.

"*Khumbula.*"

Bibi waited, afraid to reply. Another spell? More Arbor Guardian magic?

It must be. Her mom would fix everything.

Still—

Nothing happened.

Bibi waited some more. Nan opened her eyes. "Acorn," she whispered. "Don't you—feel anything?"

The *khumbula* spell hadn't worked. "What *should* I feel?" Bibi said.

Nan scratched her chin, mumbling to herself. "We'll try again later. We have to go to Splitwood now."

With great determination, she pushed herself to her feet, and spoke to Bibi in a low voice. "Quietly, Acorn—grab as many flowers as you can. Some for you, and some for me. They will keep us safe in the Tunnel Rocks. Go on!"

But before Bibi could move, Valmyr moaned. An icy fear passed through her as he began rising to his feet.

"Mom!" she whispered. Nan touched her shoulder, signaling her to stay motionless.

Once upright, Valmyr gazed vacantly around the cave with his white-filmed eyes, and long ropes of saliva hanging from his teeth. But he did not react to Bibi's presence.

Blind, she realized. Falanthrow poisoning had blinded the king of the lions.

Lashing his tail, Valmyr put one massive paw forward—then drew it back, sensing the flower-strewn floor. "What do I smell among these disgusting flowers?" he growled.

Eek hunched down, fur prickly, tail undulating behind her. "Excuse me, Lord Valmyr!" she said, raising her voice, but still clinging to the cave floor. "It is only I, the black catling."

Valmyr grinned—and then unleashed an earthquake of thunderous laughter that, even in his weakened state, seemed to make the mountain shake. "Do you hear that, Arbor Guardian? The black catling is back! That must mean—"

"The Arbor Guardian is not here, Lord Valmyr," Eek said.

The king of the lions paused, cocking his head. "Not here? Where is she?"

Eek turned to nod at Bibi. Hoping her cat knew what she was doing, Bibi got down on shaking hands and knees. Ignoring the flowers closest to Valmyr, she began scooping up the ones from other parts of the cave floor—as Nan held the branch out once more, concentrating, keeping the flowers alive. A slight quiver appeared in the Arbor Guardian's arm, and perspiration on her brow.

Eek turned back to Valmyr and let out a sad meow. "My lord, the Arbor Guardian has vanished."

The king snorted at the cave air. "What? *What!*" He growled. "Then we attack!" He tried to step forward again, but there were too many flowers. "*Agh!*" He coughed violently.

"No, my Lord! It is too dangerous."

"Hurry, Acorn!" Nan whispered. Her arm wavered with the weight of the branch.

Bibi folded the bottom of her shirt into a makeshift bowl and gathered as many flowers as she could carry. She stuck some behind her ears and entwined some in her hair. The scent made her nose itch. Returning to her mom, she offered her the rest. Nan put flowers in the pockets of her cloak and tucked some in her braids.

"Leave it to Gorka and Alenka, my lord," Eek said. "They have the Arbor Guardian's daughter. They will stop Nan Blundermuss. When she's dead, you can come out again."

Valmyr made a gurgling noise like a kettle beginning to boil. "Arbor Guardian!" He shook, every inch a violent rage. "Let me kill her myself!"

Nan pointed silently toward the cave entrance. Shielded by

Falanthrow flowers, she and Bibi locked arms, and began moving, keeping their distance from the fuming Trolliclawian king.

"Most revered Lord Valmyr," Eek said, her voice a forced calm as she slowly backed away too. "I must go. I will return when it is safe for you to come out."

Be careful, Eek . . . be careful . . .

Bibi thought she saw something new pass into Valmyr's eyes, even under their white film. He tensed his body, until his breath seemed to hover in the cave, like a specter—his next words quiet, slow, relentless.

"Black catling, I have just one more question."

Something hard cracked under Bibi's sneaker. Peering down, she noticed white sticks littered among the flowers.

Eek had almost reached Nan and Bibi. "Yes, Lord Valmyr?"

Bibi gasped. Beneath her sneaker—not sticks. Bones. Lion bones. Her heart beat faster. She thought of the lions in the atrium. She thought of the middens.

Valmyr hissed. "*Why are the flowers not making you sick?*"

There was a roar, and a yowl, and Bibi spun around.

Her heart squeezed tight—for Valmyr had lunged across the flowered floor and pinned Eek under his paw.

CHAPTER FORTY-ONE:
It's War

"Eek!" Bibi shrieked. All the times her cat had disappeared came slamming back to her. Eek, lost in the forest back in Oregon. Eek, lost in Falanthrow Forest. Eek, lost to Gorka and Alenka. And now this, worst of all.

But Nan moved before Bibi could—scrambling across the cave floor with her remaining strength until she pressed a handful of flowers against Valmyr's nose with one hand, holding the branch high with the other.

"Don't you dare!" she said, in her old woman's voice. "*Don't . . . you . . . dare!*"

There was an awful gagging sound, as the surprised Trolliclawian king, choking on Falanthrow pollen, spat and gurgled through his red teeth and froth-foamed lips.

"*Grrpphh!*" Valmyr said. "*Cchhth!*"

Bibi at last found her wits and stumbled forward—but Nan shook her head. "Stay back, Acorn!" she demanded.

Eek squirmed under the lion's paw. Nan pressed the flowers harder. Valmyr snorted and buckled. He scrambled back—Nan moving with him, keeping the flowers against his nose and mouth—until he was pinned to the wall of the cave.

"*Mrow!*" Freed, Eek darted to Bibi, who hugged her with all her might—as if she would never let her go again.

They both watched in horror as the light dimmed behind Valmyr's white-coated eyes, and the surge of flower poison worked its way through his system. Nan pressed the flowers again, and he began to shake, his red teeth rattling.

"*Agghhth!*"

The king spasmed violently against the cave wall. He made a sound like the life was being wrung from him. He collapsed to his belly and stopped moving.

Bibi and Eek and Nan stood in the cave, breathing the close air—suffused with the scent of iron and bile, and mixed with the sweet, harsh, deadly odor of the Falanthrows. They waited.

The king of the white lions remained still.

Nan began swaying on her feet drunkenly, the branch limp in one hand. "Dead," she muttered. She dropped her flowers with the other hand and crumpled to her knees like a pile of old clothes.

"Mom!" Bibi lunged forward, reaching out with her free arm.

Still conscious but clearly in pain, Nan was already struggling to her feet again, tucking her branch in her cloak. "I'm going to get you out of here!" Bibi said. Setting Eek down, Bibi took her mom's arm. After one last glance at the downed king, the three of them headed for the tunnel leading to the atrium.

They moved slowly, following the atrium light toward the shaft Bibi and Eek had used earlier.

New noises came from the atrium. Two of the Trolliclawians who had been there before were near the tunnel entrance, facing out. They watched as a crowd of other white lions raced past—too many to count. The pads of the runners' paws made a steady thumping over the rock floor.

Something big was happening. Bibi guided her weakened mom over to the tunnel wall, where the shadows were deepest. They hid against the cool stone, as Eek lurked stealthily at their feet.

One of the running lions scrambled to a stop in front of the tunnel opening, while his comrades continued scurrying past. Bibi leaned forward to listen.

"What are you waiting for, brothers?" the newcomer said, looking at the original two.

"Why shouldn't we wait?" one of them shot back. "We have nowhere to be."

"Don't you know?" The other's tail coiled and uncoiled. "Gorka and Alenka are dead! The Alala are attacking! With horns and hooves!" He growled. "Join us."

"But the Arbor Guardian! She would kill King Valmyr if she knew!"

The three of them peered toward Valmyr's cave, like prying wraiths. Bibi drew her mom deeper into the shadows, trying to stay out of sight. She swallowed, hard.

"It can't be helped," said the first lion, as they turned away again. "It's war. There are no rules in war. Are you with us or not?"

After a pause, the three Trolliclawians hissed at each other—a rallying cry—and ran off to join the group.

When they were gone, Bibi pointed toward the shaft. "Now!" she said.

CHAPTER FORTY-TWO:
Spellbreaking

Nan was too tired to pull herself through the shaft, so Bibi used all her strength to drag her by the arms, while Eek went ahead to scout for lions. But they eventually got out of the Tunnel Rocks without seeing another Trolliclawian.

In a new canyon, under the late afternoon sun, Eek found a saucer-shaped pool of cold rainwater in one of the boulders. Bibi helped her mom to her knees so they could drink. Her arms ached with the effort. Eek paused to forcefully groom herself, as if she couldn't stand the memory of Valmyr's touch.

After lifting the water to her lips with wizened hands, Nan leaned against Bibi, eyes closed. The flowers in their hair were wilting.

"Mom?" Bibi said. Being away from the gloom of the Tunnel Rocks made Nan's frailty even more pronounced. It was frightening to see her this way—what had happened to the mighty Nan Blundermuss? If her Arbor Guardian power was lost, did that mean she would never stop the lions? Would they never find Dad? Would they never go home?

Nan opened her glassy eyes, clutching at the branch in her cloak.

"*Khumbula*," she coughed.

Bibi frowned. The word from earlier. "What does that mean, Mom?"

Nan sighed unhappily. "I'm trying to right a wrong."

"We should keep moving," Eek said, standing and sniffing at the air. She pointed with her nose. "You said we have to go to Splitwood. Falanthrow Forest is that way. I'll go ahead, and make sure the path is clear."

"Don't you want to rest, Mom?" Bibi said.

But Nan rose to her feet again, and Bibi worked to keep her upright as they followed Eek through the cold afternoon light.

Bibi and Nan walked for a while in silence, as Eek, impatient, got farther and farther ahead.

Bibi thought of her nightmare. She thought of the dead trees, with their black bark. She did not want to go back to Falanthrow Forest. She could feel her hylophobia growing again. It would be worse than before. How could she explain to her mom—an Arbor Guardian—her fear of trees? She concentrated on her steps, and her breath. *Inhale. Exhale.*

Nan's next words came in a hush.

"Acorn, I want to tell you—"

Immediately, something gripped her, and she stopped, gritting her teeth and choking for air. In a snap, her already wilting flowers grayed all over, and her hair turned almost white. Bibi's flowers grayed too, disintegrating into dust.

Bibi froze, eyes searching. "Mom!" she said, bracing to support her. "What is it?"

But whatever held Nan swiftly let her go. She relaxed, though her brow remained creased in pain. Cautiously, she spoke again: "Acorn—"

The strange invisible force seized her again, and again she doubled over. "Aghh!" she cried, stomping her foot against the canyon floor in frustration.

Bibi trembled, helpless and confused and frightened. "Mom! You want to tell me *what?*"

In a moment, the unknown thing let Nan go again, and she stood there trying to catch her breath. "I can't tell you . . . what I need to tell you," she said, lifting each word like it was a heavy stone. "There's a spell on you, Acorn, and it won't let me . . ."

"A *spell?* On *me?*" Bibi looked down at herself. She didn't see any signs of enchantment. She looked the same as always, only dirtier.

They stood in the canyon—Bibi trembling, Nan fuming, and Eek waiting up ahead. Clouds moved in, making the air colder.

"You have to . . . remember it yourself," Nan continued, staring at the ground as her body slumped. "Break the spell . . . everything else will follow."

177

Bibi's head hurt. "Remember *what*? Break *what* spell?"

The seizure came back, and Nan gritted her teeth again. "Killing Valmyr . . . took the last of my power," she said, choking out the words, crouched over. "I am . . . failing. You must think of . . . when you last saw Dad." She winced.

Bibi's mind raced. When she last saw Dad? But . . .

She couldn't remember. *Why* couldn't she remember? Everything she knew about her parents seemed all of a sudden second-hand—told to her by someone else. What had happened to her memory of them? Why did she only know they had vanished?

Hand trembling, she took the photograph from her pocket. Seeing it, Nan gave a little cry. Bibi stared at her dad's goggles and lab coat and axe as she labored to hold her mom up.

Goggles. Lab coat. Axe. Why couldn't she remember anything else?

She turned the photo over. "Does it have something to do with *Praetor Wight*? Or *Anaspiritus*?"

Nan's breath grew faint. She teetered. "Close your eyes. Tell me what you see."

And because Bibi could not think what else to do, she did.

CHAPTER FORTY-THREE:
Bibi's Memory

With her eyes closed, Bibi's mind was a kinetoscope of images—flickering in black and white. Nan leaned against her, breath uneven.

"What . . . do you . . . see?" she asked.

Bibi concentrated—harder than she ever had. Harder than for any test in school. Harder than all the times she tried to distract herself from the trees with thoughts of something else. She concentrated so hard that her temples began to throb.

And the memory started to come.

She recognized it right away. It was how her nightmares always began. It was so simple: how could she have forgotten?

"The school bus is dropping me off," she said.

Nan shivered.

"I'm in the driveway," Bibi continued, voice quaking, eyes still closed.

"It's a bleak day in September," Nan said. "The trees are already losing their leaves."

Bibi closed her eyes tighter, with the weight of her mom's body against hers, in the cold of the still canyon.

"I don't see Eek," she said, wrestling with the words as she re-lived the moment. "She must be in the house. And there's something by the trees."

Her mouth went dry as she remembered turning toward the forest. *What* was by the trees?

"It's a man!" she said.

But *was* it a man? No. It moved like a man, lumbering through the forest. But it was too tall—as tall as a telephone pole, almost as tall as the other trees. And silent as fog.

Bibi heard her voice hollow out. "It's a *monster*," she said, "made of wood."

"Yes," Nan said, bobbing her head so Bibi would continue.

Bibi went deeper into the memory. The tall monster looked out upon the forest with a single gnarled eye. Its clawlike branches reached to the sky with a sudden loud *tok, tok, tok*—a sound so clear in Bibi's mind that a tingle traveled the back of her neck. Could the monster be here in the canyon too? She opened her eyes.

There was no one else in the canyon. The air carried a hint of frost, and the clouds slid along, like a gray sheet being pulled across the sky, until they hid the sun. Eek was still far ahead on the path.

"Acorn," Nan said, urgency building in her voice. "What else do you see?" Her breath, visible in the cold, remained weak, but with a more regular rhythm.

As soon as Bibi closed her eyes again, she remembered more—and this time, the memory came hard and fist-like, slamming into her stomach. There he was!

"Dad!" she cried. "The giant wooden monster is fighting Dad!" She saw him as clearly as if he was standing in front of her. The goggles. The lab coat. The axe.

But why!

She shook her head and body, trying to fling the horrible memory away. It clung like a nettle. She could hear her dad's deep voice as he yelled at the thing towering over him—the thing trying to crush him to death with its clawlike branches. *Tok, tok, tok.*

Nan spoke louder and faster, as Bibi continued shaking. "The thing with Dad is a tree wight. The first tree wight: Praetor Wight. Tree wights are zombie trees—warriors of Anaspiritus. The enemy."

Anaspiritus. The enemy. Bibi stopped, trying to digest her mom's words. *Praetor Wight.* The thing from her nightmares. The hylophobia. The writing on the photo.

Had she really been afraid of trees all this time? Or had she been afraid of the tree-like monster that attacked her dad? *A tree wight.* How could she have forgotten that, except in her nightmares? Why hadn't the writing on the photo reminded her?

Just when she nearly stopped shaking, the memory resumed,

181

like someone restarting a paused movie. In it, the screen door clattered, and Grandma Ivy—bracelets rattling, white hair pushed back with a headband—hobbled out onto the front porch, shouting at Bibi to turn away.

But Bibi could not turn away. She cried out again.

"It's taking Dad! It's flying away!" Praetor Wight soared, like a wooden ghoul in the air, her dad crumpled under one of its arms. Bibi was going to be sick—she doubled over. "Is Dad dead? Did Praetor Wight kill him?"

Nan, growing stronger, pulled her back up.

"*No*," she said, soft but firm. "Stay with the memory. You're almost at the end. What happened next?"

Bibi heard another voice in her head.

"It's . . . you," she said, listening. "Mom! You're on a tree, and it's . . . growing into the sky, like a rocket." She thought of the day she had gone into the forest next to her house to save Eek from the bees. "The sapling. The Ash tree!"

The memory clouded, and the frost condensed in the air. Regaining her composure, Bibi opened her eyes and leaned toward her mom, smelling her clothes and hair, laced with the sweet, tangy scent of dirt from home. "You shouted something to Grandma Ivy," she said. "Wh-what did you shout?"

Her mom lowered her eyes. The cold gray sky hung heavy above her.

The memory cleared again. "What did you shout?" Bibi said again, listening in her mind. She tried to repeat it. "*Uk . . . uk . . . ?*"

Nan nodded. "*Ukhohlwe*," she whispered—delicately, as if the word might cut her tongue.

182

"What—what does that mean?" Bibi asked.

And then, like blood rushing into a neglected limb, she knew.

"*You* made me forget! You cast a spell on my memory! *Ukhohlwe* means *forget!*"

Nan's aged body drooped, as she let Bibi's words linger in the frigid air. She spoke softly. "*We* made you forget. Your grandmother made the spell, when she was still an Arbor Guardian too. Disguised it, as medicine."

Grandma Ivy? The bottle of anti-anxiety pills on the bathroom counter. *I'm calling to make sure you take your pill this morning, dear.*

The tears burned Bibi's cheeks. "But *why?*"

"We were trying to protect you."

Bibi jerked back, hands balled into fists. "From *what?*"

Nan's eyes shimmered. "You were too young to know. I wanted you to forget what you had seen—you weren't supposed to see it. We kept it from you since you were a child. Too dangerous! I didn't want you to find out who you were." She paused, kneading her hands. "Dad and I thought we could handle the danger by ourselves. We were wrong. I'm so sorry, Acorn."

Bibi frowned again, eyes stinging. The *Ukhohlwe* spell had made her forget—and forgetting had somehow made her afraid. More afraid than she would have been if she had known. All those times she had asked about her past. About the family. *I didn't want you to find out who you were . . .*

Gossamer snow began to speckle down from the slate-gray sky, with flurries like slow-falling stars. The cold air hung so still that Bibi could hear the flakes hitting the rocks in a quiet sizzle. Yet a strange heat, tinged with pins and needles, suffused her body.

"What about Dad?" she stammered, thinking back to the fight with Praetor Wight. "Where is he? Is he here?"

Looking back at Bibi, Nan's eyes were full. "He's closer than you think," she said. "Don't you feel it, too? You've broken the spell, Acorn."

Closer? Where? Bibi started to look around, when something else happened. She gasped, staring at her mom in disbelief. Somehow, in the blink of an eye, Nan had shed her old age, like dead skin. She was young again.

"Mom! What happened to you!"

Nan glanced at her hands, as the dusting of snow thickened. She flexed her fingers and bent her arms, as if noticing them for the first time. Her eyes sparkled, and her braids were dark. The flowers at her feet blazed bright red-orange.

Beaming, Nan took Bibi's face in her hands. "You see? My sweet girl. My Acorn. Thank you." She kissed her forehead. "You broke *ukhohlwe*, the memory spell, by remembering what happened, and remembering who you are. You restored my power. Now we can do what needs to be done."

"I don't under—" Bibi began.

But Nan grabbed her by the hand, and, full of new vitality, led her off into the snow, cloak flapping behind. Eek, up ahead, saw that they were moving again, and turned and led the way farther into the canyon.

Bibi struggled to keep pace with her mom's long gait. She couldn't speak, gulping at the cold air.

"Dad came here to fight his battle." Nan's voice quavered slightly. "We'll meet him in the center of Falanthrow Forest—in Splitwood—where we'll fight ours."

She squeezed Bibi's hand as they continued forward. Bibi held on, still confused. *His battle. Our battle.*

"But how did you get young again?"

Nan smiled.

"Arbor Guardians are symbiotic," she said. "We nurture and magnify power in one another. We are deeply linked. I didn't appreciate that until I came here, and almost lost everything. That's why I sent the bees for you, Acorn, after your grandmother renounced her own power. I shouldn't have left Oregon without you. And if you hadn't come . . ."

The warmth in Bibi pulsed, and the pins and needles prickled. She remembered the rain in the forest next to their house. How she almost refused to climb the Ash sapling.

"You *saved* me, Acorn," Nan said. "Now we go to Splitwood, to save the Falanthrows, and find Dad, and go home." She stood taller as they walked. "One Arbor Guardian can only do so much. But two Arbor Guardians together? *That's* power."

Bibi crinkled her brow. "You found another Arbor Guardian?"

She half-expected to see Grandma Ivy hiding among the canyon's white-capped rocks. But if Grandma Ivy had renounced her own power . . .

Nan laughed—a sound like bright butterflies in the snow.

Suddenly Bibi knew what the *Ukhohlwe* spell really hid, and what the warm pins and needles really meant.

185

I didn't want you to find out who you were.

"Yes," Nan said. "I found another Arbor Guardian. I found you."

CHAPTER FORTY-FOUR:
The Battle of Falanthrow Forest

The rock floor seemed to crack open beneath Bibi. "*Me?*" she said. "An Arbor Guardian?" Impossible. *She* couldn't save the trees. She had hylophobia!

Before Nan could say more, Eek came charging toward them from the other end of the canyon—crossing the distance in seconds, and meowing loudly. "Come quick! Up ahead, there's—"

She stopped short, taken back by Nan's changes.

While Nan hastily explained what had happened, the snow fell harder. Bibi squinted. In front of them, the canyon opened onto the scree-covered slope. Beyond that, Falanthrow Forest loomed—a wide inky blot against the white-flecked air. She felt her knees wobble. Could she really go back there?

A faraway rumble unsettled the calm, like flies pricking the surface of a lake. "What's that noise?" Nan said.

"It's what I wanted to tell you," Eek said. "The Alala! Hurry!"

"Is Dad there?" Bibi couldn't control the shaking in her voice as they moved off again.

They ran the rest of the way through the canyon—to where its walls had weathered away—and began crossing the slope. The snow teemed, and Bibi could see her panting breath in the bitter air. She tried to block out what her mom had said earlier and focus on what was ahead. But her mind kept buffeting her, like the wind in the yard on the day she had come here, blowing back with the same questions.

How could she be an Arbor Guardian? Had she always been?

At the edge of the forest, they stopped, looking in at the black Falanthrows. On the tree branches, the snow accumulated in lines like white serpents. Beneath that, icicles already hung like fangs. The rumbling sound grew louder, from the right.

"The Alala are coming," Eek said. "Just wait." She made anxious figure eights in the snow as Nan remained quiet and still, watching.

Bibi couldn't stop thinking of the forest. *Hylophobia is sometimes prompted by the mere sight of a tree*, her book had said, *and made worse by physical contact with one*. And yet here, she felt nothing from even the closest Falanthrow . . . close enough to touch. What if—did she dare? She looked at her mom, and then back at the closest Falanthrow.

The last time she touched a tree, it felt awful. Now, she took a deep breath, extending a hand . . . closer . . . closer . . .

There.

Bibi raised her eyebrows. The black bark was cold and stony

188

on the tips of her fingers. But it did not make her nauseous or dizzy. It felt like nothing but tree.

She placed her palm flat on the trunk. Not pleasant—but not repulsive, either.

How could that be? Because of the breaking of the memory spell? Was the hylophobia really gone? Was she really an Arbor Guardian? She still felt wrong—like she had ended up in someone else's body. Her mom had transformed—had she transformed, too? The warm pins and needles that had begun in the canyon still lingered in her chest and arms and belly.

The rumbling sound roared, and Bibi turned to the right. She reared back in surprise as a herd of hundreds of elk clamored past, turning off the Circle Road and heading toward the forest, panting and snorting, like a freight train in the soft snow. They were mostly adults—mostly bigger than Corineus and the others. Broad-shouldered stags with wide battle-axe antlers. Lean, muscular does with powerful kicking legs.

The Alala.

They moved with a single purpose, machine-like into the dead forest. Bibi felt their body heat as they passed. But they did not stop at the sight of Bibi and Eek and Nan. Eek hissed and Nan waved her arms. "Wait!" she said. The grim, dogged elk continued thundering by, drowning out her voice with their hooves.

"We are the Arbor Guardians!" Nan shouted. "We will save the forest! The lions will leave! You don't need to go to war!"

The Alala kept running. Bibi could not see her friends among them. No Corineus or Genza. No Aruna or Baranji. As they got farther away, the elk began chanting in unison. It was hard to hear what they were saying at first. But as Bibi listened, it got clearer, and she remembered.

"Antlers and hooves will beat the white lions," the Alala said as they ran. "Antlers and hooves will beat the white lions." Over and over.

The last of the herd passed. The snow and Harrowing mist closed in upon the Alala as they got farther into the forest. Bibi glanced at her mom, who fumed, frustration on her face. "Fools!" Nan said. "If they had only waited!"

And the lions?

Bibi watched—and just before the Alala disappeared completely into the white and black, she saw the Trolliclawians at last. Everywhere at once. They had been waiting in the dead trees, camouflaged by the snow.

They dove down like swooping ghosts. Hundreds of lions diving on hundreds of elk. Some lions broke the elk backs as they landed. Some attached themselves teeth-first to the soft undersides of elk necks, clamping until the warm blood gushed. The elk stabbed and punched with antlers and hooves. Everywhere, the white snow spotted red.

The Battle of Falanthrow Forest had begun.

CHAPTER FORTY-FIVE:
No Ordinary Snow

"Acorn!" Nan's voice cut through the battle din. "We have to go around them. Come on! We have to get to Splitwood. We have to stop this!"

Everywhere, the blood in the snow. Bibi felt sick in her stomach again.

They moved along the outskirts of the forest. When they could no longer see or hear the battle, they entered.

The weather grew worse, and, with no leaves to slow its descent, the snow condensed in deep dunes among the trees. On the forest path, it already drifted up around Bibi's shins. She still couldn't believe she no longer had hylophobia, but the difficulty of each step kept her from the question for a while. Eek moved in little hops, trying in vain to keep her paws warm and dry. Bibi picked her up and held her close, and the cat yowled through chattering teeth.

"We'll find Dad soon, Acorn," Nan said, urging them on, Wellingtons crunching through the snow. "But first we need to save the Falanthrows—all the Falanthrows. The best place to do that is the middle of the forest—Splitwood. You're almost ready. Your first spell."

Bibi wanted more than anything to find her dad. But a spell? Her first spell? Arbor Guardian or not, she knew nothing about magic. "Don't I need lessons?"

Nan smiled—reaching into her cloak and producing another, shorter branch. She held it out.

"I almost forgot. I've been saving this. I should have given it to you sooner."

Bibi's eyes widened. A branch—*her* branch? She took it in her free hand, feeling it warm and smooth against her numb fingers, like driftwood heated in the sun. The snowflakes melted as they hit it, and its ridges fit her palm perfectly—as if she had been born holding it.

"But—I don't know how to use this," Bibi stammered.

Nan stopped, smiling again. "You do. Don't you feel the pins and needles?"

Bibi nodded. The pins and needles feeling that had started in the canyon sizzled in her chest and seemed to dance around the wood she held in her hand. How did her mom know?

"Your Arbor Guardian magic," Nan said. "You'll know how

to use it when we cast our spell—when we get to Splitwood. You'll find it on your own."

On your own.

No. She couldn't do that. Unless . . .

Opening the side door during the storm, running into the forest next to their house, climbing the sapling. That was what her mom meant, wasn't it? Maybe Bibi had already been on her own without even realizing it.

Soon it was hard to see anything at all. It was as if they were moving through a downpour of white confetti. On the path, the snow came up to Bibi's knees. Some of the trees were buried nearly to their bottom branches.

"H-h-how will we find Splitwood in this strange snow?" Eek said miserably, teeth still chattering.

Nan peered into the icy wind. "Strange snow . . ." she said, as if noticing it for the first time. She shielded her face with her hand.

She stopped again—this time abruptly. Stopping too, Bibi followed her gaze, trying to see what had gotten her attention. There was nothing but dead trees and an impenetrable veil of white. "Mom?"

"Strange snow . . ." Nan repeated. She lowered her hand from her face, revealing a furrowed brow. She caught a few fat flakes in her palm and peered down to read them like tea leaves.

After a moment's study, she closed her hand in a fist, and her voice dropped to a quiet fury. "Praetor Wight!" Without waiting, she headed into the snow again, faster.

"Wait!" Bibi cried, still struggling to keep up, imagining new horrors ahead. That name again. "What about Praetor Wight?"

Nan set her jaw, and for a while, said nothing as they trudged on. Finally:

"This is no ordinary snow, Acorn. This is tree wight magic. That means Praetor Wight is still alive."

Bibi felt a tremor go through her, as she clung to Eek like a good-luck charm. "I don't understand."

Nan drew her cloak tighter around her with each stride.

"Remember what you saw? How the wight and Dad were fighting?" She brushed the snow out of her braids. "We had known it was coming for him. He was ready when it came. He planned to kill it."

Bibi's mouth fell open. "To *kill* it?" She thought of the telephone-pole size monster towering over her dad. How it had brutally clutched him. Was killing a thing like that even possible? A knot of sickness returned to her belly. "But if Praetor Wight is still alive—what about Dad?"

For a heartbeat, Nan's eyes were colored by something Bibi had never seen there before. Then she forced them into a calm, as if molding a clay mask. "He would not want us to worry. We have to hurry to Splitwood. We have to hope, Acorn."

Bibi studied her mom's face through the falling sheets of white and realized what had entered her eyes so briefly. Fear. Nan Blundermuss, the mighty Arbor Guardian, was afraid.

Soon, the light dimmed, and night fell.

From her cloak, Nan produced a sprig of *Photinus foliosa*—a faint torch in the snow-swept murk. The Harrowing mist pressed against them like the palm and fingers of a closing fist. Where the light ended, the forest waited, deep and black as the Cosmos.

Bibi, head pounding with worry, held her branch close with one hand, and her cat with the other. She peered ahead, trying to find the tree with two trunks. Her mind became sluggish with the cold, and every step through the deep drifts took more determination than the one before.

"Are we close?" she said when she could no longer feel her feet in her sneakers.

"We're close," Nan said. Her shoulders quaked with cold—or it might have been fear again.

Eek curled into a black ball in the crook of Bibi's arm—eyes screwed shut, breath shallow. Bibi covered her with the front of her jacket. She could protect Eek, she knew. But could she protect the forest, too? She bit her lip, her face seared by the whinging wind. Did the fate of the Alala really depend on her? She wondered if the battle still raged. The blood in the snow . . .

Something ahead made her heart stop—a white beast, arms flexed like a warrior. "Mom!" she whispered. Eek opened one eye. Nan turned and tensed, raising her light.

No—not a beast. The two-trunked tree, draped in a coat of snow. Splitwood! They had made it. And . . . something else. "Listen," Nan said. "Do you hear that?"

"Is it Dad?" Bibi said, straining her ears. *Please be Dad.*

Beneath the white noise of the snow, a crunching sound. Muffled voices, too.

A plodding form emerged from the white-out—and Bibi's heart sank. Not her dad, but a stag, with broad, magnificent antlers and a scruffy coat. A pair of ragged scars ran across one of his sides, and he snorted angry steam from flared nostrils.

Bibi could hardly see. The stag leaned forward, taking a few more steps through the sheets of white, and bringing his long face a few feet from her mom's. Nan held her ground, and with her branch in front of her, read his expression, as his eyes hardened into a glare.

She pushed Bibi behind her, protectively.

"Genza!"

CHAPTER FORTY-SIX:
The Meeting in Splitwood

Genza! Bibi trembled. He had aged since the incident at the River Eldred, and now appeared as a battle-hardened adult—taller, with broader, sharper, bloodstained antlers, jutting out like the branches of the dead Falanthrows. A warrior woodskull.

Did he still feel betrayed, as he had on that day so long ago? The small ball of fur in Bibi's arms bristled, as a growl curdled within Eek.

But Genza spoke with a soft voice, and the glare faded from his eyes.

"So it *is* you, Arbor Guardian. And Bibi Blundermuss! Hard to see in this storm, eh? Careful—the lions are near."

Nan didn't move, except to dart her eyes at the wall of white around them. "Are there other elk with you?"

Genza opened his mouth to respond, when a shadow

appeared to his left—a full-grown golden-orange doe, also half-sunk in the snow. Aruna! And then another, smaller elk, with deep, sad eyes, and a tuft of black hair. Bibi's heart melted. *Corineus.*

Aruna beamed, brightening the gloom. "Arbor Guardian! Bibi Blundermuss!"

"Hello, friends," Nan said, her voice cracking in the cold. Cautiously, she lowered her branch.

Corineus's eyes met Bibi's. "I knew you would find her," he said—his words warm despite his chattering teeth. The cold wind on Bibi's face made it hard to smile, but a mighty happiness rose inside her at the sight of her friend, and she hugged him tightly with one arm, still holding Eek in the other.

"Hold on," Corineus said. Another shadow emerged. A second doe, a little bigger than Aruna. Sleek and streamlined, with eyes like black river rocks.

Nan gasped. "Yega-Woo! And . . ."

Her voice trailed off as she covered her mouth.

Bibi felt like she was back on the tree-rocket, but this time with a surge of joy. A man sat on Yega-Woo's back. He wore a familiar white lab coat, torn and grimy. There were ice-encrusted goggles pushed back on top of his head, and an axe in the belt at his side. His skin, nearly as pale as the snow, was accented by a disheveled black beard. He smelled of grease and gears and stardust.

Bjorn Skovgaard. Dad. Bibi couldn't move or speak.

Bjorn, seemingly snow-blind, dismounted. Almost before his feet were on the ground, Nan embraced him with a forcefulness that emptied his lungs, making him laugh even as he groaned. *"Min elskede!"* he said. She released him happily, and he gazed at her, taking her face in his hands. "Ah, but you're a sight for sore eyes! Let me bask in your glow awhile."

At first, she did—then she shook her head. "There'll be time enough, dear Bjorn," she said, her voice light as a filigree of frost. "There's someone else to see you, too."

He peered into the sea of white. "Ah, the little elk told me—Beebs?"

Bibi, obscured by the cataract of snow, still couldn't move or speak for happiness. Her eyes flooded; she did not care that the tears froze on her cheeks.

When Bjorn saw her, he strode to her side in two steps, greeting her with a huge hug. She clung to him, burying her face in his lab coat. "Hello, Beebs," he said again and again—as if repeating her name would shield her from the cold. Bibi sobbed, and Eek purred, and Nan put her arms around them all. And the family was whole again.

CHAPTER FORTY-SEVEN:
What Happened to Bjorn

Despite the storm, and despite the dead trees and the Battle of Falanthrow Forest, Bibi would have been happy to stay there forever, in the arms of both parents again at last. For the first time in a long time, she let her mind be calm. No more worrying about her loved ones, or things she didn't understand. No more pressure to face a nightmarish fear or be something she wasn't. No more watching things happen out of her control. Just be, and let the tears fall.

But beyond Corineus and the frosted, smiling elk, something moved in the storm. Beyond the two-trunked tree, the closest Falanthrows leaned, as if grappling to free themselves from the cold ground. Bibi blinked. A trick of the light? An errant snow-gust?

Before she could ask, Genza spoke—his voice slowly

regaining its old bell-like clang. "Many of the Alala have fallen, Arbor Guardian—we were overrun with lions almost as soon as the battle began. Baranji was with us, but we became separated. We escaped only because of the snow. Only by luck did we make it to Splitwood—to home."

Nan bowed her head somberly. "I see." She turned to Bjorn. "And what happened to you, dear Bjorn? Where have you been?"

Bjorn straightened, brushing the snow from his beard. "*Min elskede*, I'm only alive because of Yega-Woo. She saved me."

There was a pause as everyone turned toward the doe with the black river-rock eyes. Genza nudged her. "Go on, Sweet Yega-Woo. Tell them what happened, eh?"

Yega-Woo nodded, and cleared her throat.

"After the ambush, I lured Valmyr away, through the forest—past the Circle Road, past the Tunnel Rocks, and into the mountains. There, I lost him."

Genza smiled. "So Yega-Woo saved my life, too. Valmyr would have killed me."

Yega-Woo went on. "I never ran so fast or far. After Valmyr gave up, I needed rest. In the mountains, I found a cave—I went in and fell into a deep sleep. When I woke, I heard fighting."

Bjorn put one hand on his axe.

"That was Praetor Wight and me. We'd been fighting for months. A harder fight than I expected—a real battle royale."

"Is it as I suspected, Bjorn?" Nan said, searching his eyes. "Is Praetor Wight still alive? Has it conjured this snow?"

Bjorn rubbed his head. "Yes." He sighed. "I'm sorry, *min*

elskede. I wore the beast down but could not kill it. I gave it everything. The Wight Slayer failed."

Bibi looked at her mom, and then back at her dad. "The Wight Slayer?"

Bjorn unholstered his axe, holding it up so she could see. The blade was pockmarked with dents, but it gleamed in the dim light. "This, Beebs. I made it specially, to kill Praetor Wight." He grinned beneath his beard. "You see, there's no spell to stop a fully-formed tree wight. You have to chop it down. But it is one of the densest creatures in the Cosmos, so you need an especially strong blade." He sighed again. "The Wight Slayer was not strong enough. I must have struck Praetor Wight a thousand times. A *hundred* thousand! Nothing. I was trapped. Ah! I've been in some tough spots in my life, but I've never been so close to death."

Yega-Woo shook her coat to remove a layer of snow. She continued: "From the cave, I saw Bjorn Skovgaard in trouble. I whispered—*I am the fastest elk in the forest. Get on.*"

"And I did." Bjorn smiled, remembering. "Never thought I'd meet a creature who could outrun a tree wight. Fastest elk in the forest? Yega-Woo, I'd wager you're the fastest elk in the Cosmos."

He ran a hand over her hide fondly, and she stood tall, like a marble statue in the snow. Bibi wanted to hug her. *You saved my Dad,* she wanted to shout. *He's alive because of you.* Nan said: "Yega-Woo, we owe you more than we can repay."

The doe did not reply, and Bjorn, acknowledging her modesty with a nod, continued.

"Well, we made it down the mountain and into the forest, and found the little elk, Corineus, by luck—farther east, where the combat was." He turned to Nan. "I assured our friends that you have no allegiance to the white lions, *min elskede*—apparently, some of them had gotten the wrong impression. Corineus told me Beebs was here, too."

Bjorn adjusted his goggles. For a few seconds, no one spoke, absorbing the tale. Eek, in Bibi's arms, fidgeted against the cold.

"Listen!" Corineus said, interrupting the hush. "What's that?"

An updraft parted the curtains of snow, and the dim *Photinus* light revealed shapes moving in the forest—long, lean, close to the ground.

Everyone went still as stone. "Lions!" Genza spat the word, lowering his blood-stained antlers.

CHAPTER FORTY-EIGHT:
Praetor Wight's Army

There were ten of them, a few hundred feet in the distance, moving raggedly through the stormy darkness, perpendicular to the two-trunked tree. The Falanthrows swayed overhead, top-heavy with ice. Bibi and the others held their breath, hoping not to be seen.

Then the wind shifted, and the snow curtains closed, and the Trolliclawians were hidden again.

"Gone!" Aruna said, her voice clipping. "Did they see us?"

Nan shook her head. "I think not. But it's time to act. We must stop Praetor Wight's army."

As cold as Bibi was, a new chill went through her. Its *army?* There were *more* wights? She saw the animals' eyes cloud with worry. "What do you mean, eh?" Genza said.

Nan spoke quickly. "This is bigger than Trolliclawians and

Alala. A wight is a zombie tree. Praetor Wight, the first wight, made the Harrowing. It killed your forest in order to make *more* wights." She gestured to the nearby Falanthrows. "These dead trees, which have already put your lives in danger, will soon become even more dangerous. They will become wights too. They will kill us all—unless Bibi and I prevent it, reviving the trees with the *khula* spell: the Quickening."

As the elk absorbed this, Bjorn stepped forward, nodding vigorously, his voice deep as the snow. "Ah, let's make ourselves useful, friends. Surely there are more white lions coming—and surely the ones we saw will be back. Circle the Arbor Guardians— protect them as they work!" He hefted his axe, and without another word, sauntered some ten paces into a deep drift, facing away from the two-trunked tree.

"Dad!" Bibi cried. She extended an arm, scarcely able to see him in the thick snow. Had they come back together only to be separated again?

"Everything is going to be all right, Beebs!" he assured her, without turning around. "Listen to your mom!" He put his goggles on and held his axe shoulder-height.

After another moment's hesitation, Genza, Yega-Woo, Aruna, and even Corineus followed Bjorn's lead, spacing themselves around the two-trunked tree at even intervals, facing outward into the gloom. "This is the true Battle of Falanthrow Forest," Genza said, holding his head high as he moved through the falling snow. "Let's make it count, eh?"

Surrounded by the ring of friends, Nan turned to Bibi, smiling intently, and gesturing to the two-trunked tree. "One trunk points east. One points west. I'll take one side—you, the other. Okay?"

Bibi's head hurt. Her first spell. "Half the forest! But—"

"Nan Blundermuss!" Corineus called. "The trees have started changing!"

Nan raised her *Photinus* higher, casting the Falanthrows in its eerie luminescence. The closest trees moved their branches on their own, undulating them like enormous clumps of black seaweed.

Bibi wobbled with a hint of dizziness. She wanted to run. Hylophobia again?

Nan squeezed her arm. "Face west, Acorn!"

Not hylophobia. There were bigger things to fear than the trees. Bibi raised her head, gritting her teeth, digging her fingernails into her palms. She couldn't let her friends down. She turned until she and her mom stood back-to-back beside the two-trunked tree. The warm pins and needles tingled in her chest and belly—like sap pumped by heartwood.

"*Khula*, Acorn," Nan said, over her shoulder. "The spell."

Scattered snowflakes stung Bibi's cheeks and nose. She clutched her branch in one hand, and her cat in the other, as the zombifying trees flung the ice from their upper branches, sending it cascading to the ground in a shower of shards. Genza snorted, rearing back on his hind legs.

"That's . . . it?" Bibi said. "Just . . . *khula*?"

"Gather your energy," Nan said. "Let it build. We have only one chance—saving the forest will take as much strength as we can summon." She reached back to grab Bibi's hand, with fingers that were so cold. She lowered her voice, speaking as if there was too much to say in the time left, and swaying a little where she stood. "I . . . I can't do this without you, Bibi."

Bibi couldn't remember the last time her mother called her by name. She blinked away tears. Her pins and needles shimmered inside. Her magic. She set her jaw.

"Watch out!" Yega-Woo said. The wind shifted again, changing the angle of the snowfall enough to reveal that the lions were back. They were closer—close enough to lunge at the elk and Bjorn. They began circling, as the trees reached skyward with their pike-fingers. Bibi felt goosebumps, even where she was numb.

And then she heard it. *Tok, tok, tok.*

She went rigid with fear. Standing behind the lions, and beside the undulating trees—like a sinister general with his soldiers—Praetor Wight loomed. Exactly how she had seen it six months ago, and exactly how she had seen it in her nightmares—telephone-pole size, with long, clawlike branches, and a single gnarled eye. The first zombie tree—the one that brought the Harrowing, and fought her dad, and wanted to make an army out of Falanthrow Forest.

Nan saw it too—she tensed, throwing out her next words like a lifeline.

"Have you gathered your energy, Bibi? Do you feel strong enough?"

Bibi nodded. She could barely keep the pins-and-needles feeling in. "But what about Praetor Wight, Mom? Dad said there's no spell—"

"First the forest, Bibi! Hold your branch out."

One of the lions lunged, trying to break through the line. Fast as a spark shooting across the snow, Bjorn deftly caught its side with his axe, sending it bleeding back into the dark. The elk, eyes white with terror, watched it go, and then hunched their shoulders, holding the line. The other lions circled closer, and the trees swayed, and Praetor Wight loomed, with its gnarled eye. *Tok, tok, tok.*

"*Khula*," Nan said, quickly. "Together. On three."

Bibi thought her heart might explode. She could do this. No going back. She was an Arbor Guardian. Like her mom.

"One," Nan said—rooted and firm as the trees groaned, furious at their roots frozen in the forest floor. "Hang on, Eek," Bibi whispered, extending her branch. *Hang on, Dad.*

"Two . . ."

"Be strong, friends!" Bjorn snarled, swinging his axe overhead, his lab-coat flapping around him. "We've lions and wights to stop tonight!"

The lions roared, with breath of iron and bile. Praetor Wight took a step toward the closest tree.

Bibi and her mother leaned back against each other—fortifying, resisting. Then they cried the spell word, aiming their branches toward opposite ends of the forest.

"*KHULA!*"

CHAPTER FORTY-NINE:
The Light and the Fire

The pins-and-needles energy erupted in a bright light from the end of Bibi's branch. Like a flash flood, it flowed down and over the ground, and under the elk and lions, illuminating them all from beneath.

So much light!

Beyond, Bibi's energy rose again, joining Nan's energy— making a radiant whirlwind that spun around them and into the forest, shining on the mist and snow, and the black trees.

Bibi stifled a shriek. Beyond the two-trunked tree, Praetor Wight moved from Falanthrow to Falanthrow, tearing them by the trunks from the cold ground—freeing them before the spell took hold. The unearthed zombie trees took awkward steps on long scraggly roots, like giant fawns. As they got their legs, they stomped forward, kicking up huge sprays of snow. Bjorn shouted, his axe cutting broad swathes through the air, as the elk held the line. Blade and antlers and hooves.

"The wight army is on the move, *min elskede!*"

The *khula* light strengthened. The lions paused, watching it overhead, their retinas reflecting it like burning coals. They seemed to know what was coming. They crouched in the snow, yowling at the awful, swirling magic. And they bounded away into the forest.

"The trees, Bibi!" Nan's braids and cloak fluttered in an icy gust.

Bibi gripped her branch with all her might. *Khula.* Her face—raw. The light—spreading outward, catching the closest trees as they moved, freezing them in strange, jagged shapes.

Got you! Got you! Got you! Power surged through her—more than she had ever felt. Like the trees were blades of grass she blew on. Not like a witch—like a goddess. Dazzling, intoxicating. The pins and needles effervesced in her.

The Quickening finally began. The bare black branches of the caught trees sprouted long green leaves, their twigs suddenly studded with fat buds. Like fireworks, the buds burst in blooms of orange and red. The sweet harsh Falanthrow glitter-pollen poured into the night-turned-day. Soon, the trees were laden with red-orange flowers. With a stretching sound, like something being turned inside out, their black bark ripped open, revealing new bark underneath, intricately ridged and earth-colored.

Would the magic reach all the way to the forest's edge? Bibi ground her teeth together. *Go, go, go . . .*

Only Praetor Wight did not transform. It watched the swirling light and its gnarled eye began to glow, red as an ancient star—raging as it saw its work undone. *Tok, tok, tok.* Bibi felt it pushing back—so strong, so strong.

The Arbor Guardians were strong, too. The *khula* light changed, devouring air and becoming fire. It veered like a giant bottle-rocket, incinerating the sky with white heat.

In response, Praetor Wight's gnarled eye blazed so hot it turned blue. Raising its spiky branches high, the original zombie tree whipped the storm into a new frenzy, battling the flames in the sky, pelting the forest with a deluge of snow and sleet. Soon, the storm drowned the *khula* fire, coughing up a billowing cloud of black smoke that settled over everything—trees and lions and elk and humans—until all was darkness.

Bibi couldn't see anything. Still holding Eek, she reached back, but couldn't feel anything. Nan Blundermuss was gone.

"Mom!"

Had she been swept away by the storm?

And if Bibi and her mom had saved the forest but failed to destroy Praetor Wight . . . what then?

"*MOM!*"

Something emerged from the gloom, but it was not Nan Blundermuss.

Praetor Wight. Alone with Praetor Wight.

You're on your own.

Bibi felt her throat tighten. The original zombie tree—close enough to touch. Illuminated by its gnarled eye, glowing red once more.

Bibi struggled to draw breath. In the wight's shadow, she felt so small. She clutched her branch like a sword, her fingers numb. Eek unsheathed her claws, but Bibi could feel her trembling terribly. The wight looked down at Bibi as if the worst was over and it had nothing to fear from a twelve-year-old girl. As if it was laughing at her—waiting for her to die from fright.

You won't believe what she's *scared of.*

No. Bibi refused to be scared. She set her jaw and took a deep breath, concentrating on the pins and needles in her chest—the Arbor Guardian energy. She looked up into the wight's gnarled eye and hissed: "There's no spell to stop a fully-formed wight, but I am going to stop you!"

Her power surged, becoming pure electricity in her branch-hand. With every last bit of strength, she stabbed Praetor Wight at the base of its trunk.

Bibi's branch impaled the petrified wood as easily as if it was hot wax. She retrieved it and stabbed again. With each plunge, the hole in the trunk got bigger. The zombie stood silent, but she sensed surprise and horror in the gnarled eye. She stabbed, over and over, until it flailed its pike arms.

With her last stab, she sank her branch to the fist—and the wight's limbs drooped and withered. Praetor Wight juddered and shook, and Bibi pulled her branch free, arm aching from the effort. She stumbled back, Eek still clutched under one arm. More holes burned, as if by acid, through the wight's hard stone bark. The outer layer melted away, revealing cambium tattooed with rot, spreading like a blooming bloodstain. The gnarled eye closed upon itself.

Then came an otherworldly shriek—awful, high-pitched, ear-rending, like a ghost forced to die again. And with that, Praetor Wight blew apart, in a geyser of shredded stone and wood that rained all around the smoke-filled forest—a million small meteors that hissed to oblivion in the deep, deep dark.

CHAPTER FIFTY:
The Wight Slayer

Bibi, huddled down, teeth chattering, clutched her cat and branch. Her head spun, and the last of the wight drifted away in a mulchy vapor, as the forest grew black once more.

She had done it. Praetor Wight was dead.

"Mom! Dad! Where are you?"

A small hole opened in the smoke overhead. The moon poked through, and pale light lit the forest in scattered shafts. The trees stood immersed in a frozen sea of plunging peaks and valleys, as if a winter's worth of snow had dropped in Praetor Wight's last outpouring of storm. They poked above the snow-waves, like swimmers trying not to drown. A delicate rime of ice coated their outstretched branches, making their beautiful red-orange flowers and earth-colored bark sparkle in the moonlight.

Eek fidgeted out of Bibi's arms and into the snow—her body light enough to skim across the crusted surface. She had picked up a scent. "This way, Bibi!" she said. Bibi scrambled to follow.

They found Nan first—sitting in the snow, a few hundred feet away. Dazed, but okay. Bibi helped her to her feet and hugged her tight—as if they'd been separated for a lifetime, instead of just a few minutes. "I thought I'd lost you again, Mom."

Bjorn came next, pushing his way through the deep drifts, axe at his side. His black beard was salted with frost, and his goggles so icy they hid his eyes. He dragged them to the top of his head.

"By the Cosmos, Beebs," he said, trying to catch his breath. "I saw what you did to that wight—incredible! I have never seen an Arbor Guardian do that." He took Nan's arm. "Are you okay, *min elskede*?"

"Give me a minute," Nan said. But her smile was returning.

Bjorn nodded. He said he'd look for the elk while the Arbor Guardians recovered. "I fear our friends are scattered far and wide. Can't go home without saying goodbye to them, can we?" He winked and crunched away.

Bibi watched him go, wondering how he knew they were going home.

Nan's face grew thoughtful and faraway—as if she was thinking of home too . . . of walking in the forest near their house. She looked up at the moon, shaking the snow out of her braids. "There's no spell to stop a fully-formed tree wight, Bibi," she said.

Bibi bit her lip. "I know, Mom."

"And yet you stopped it."

"I *know*, Mom."

Nan labored to articulate her next question but settled on something simple. "*How?*"

Bibi's face flushed. "I . . . I don't know. I just . . . stabbed it with my branch."

Nan's smile grew stronger. "In the war against Anaspiritus and the wights," she said, "the Arbor Guardians have told of a new kind of witch—a witch with something more than the old magic." She paused. "Do *you* feel like that kind of witch, Bibi?"

Bibi cocked her head. What a question! She shrugged, absent-mindedly making a palm-print in the snow. But the pins and needles were part of her, now.

Nan took Bibi's hand, unable to hide the awe in her face. "*Sawubona*, Bibi," she said.

CHAPTER FIFTY-ONE:
The Seedling

Within the hour, the sentinel-rays of the coming sunrise coated the forest in gray light. The smoke faded completely, and with the rising of the warming sun, the forest stuttered in a drizzle of snowmelt. Dripping water ran in rivulets down the Falanthrow trunks. Under the trees, the snow grew pockmarked with drops. The cold white hills began to dimple and sag—and, one by one, to collapse.

The early morning uncovered the forest—reborn, wet, and sparkling. The revealed, healed Falanthrows glistened in the sun, freed of ice, their red-orange flowers pouring the gingery glitter-pollen into the humid air, and filling the forest with the sound of wind chimes. Bibi and Nan's hill flattened with a *shh*, and they found themselves laughing, standing in slushy mud. Eek, fortified with more of the cat-grass antidote, perched in one of the branches of the two-trunked tree. Soon, only occasional splotches of the storm's wrath remained—a mottled patchwork of snow spots, scattered on the forest floor.

Within two hours, they heard Bjorn's boots come squishing back. Bibi's heart swelled when she saw Corineus, Yega-Woo, Genza, Aruna, Baranji—yes, Baranji, too. And others. About thirty elk she did not know. A sprinkled swarm of bees trailed them.

With slow, spent movements, the elk made a circle around the Arbor Guardians. Nan tied her braids back. Eek climbed out of the two-trunked tree and into Bibi's arms—Bibi held her close, running her hand down her wet fur, and looking at the survivors.

"Eek is our friend," she reassured them. "Not a Trolliclawian."

"Welcome, Alala," Nan said. "The forest is yours again." She looked at Bibi. "We have done what I tried to do six black moons ago." Though fatigued, Nan stood tall and strong, gripping her cloak with authority.

Genza nodded. "Thank you." He looked at the other elk—those Bibi didn't know. "These are the heroes I was telling you about, friends." The Alala, silent and huge, stared in wonder at Bibi and Nan. Genza turned to the trees. "The Falanthrows are stronger, eh, Arbor Guardian? There will be no new Harrowing. The white lions were seen fleeing into the mountains. They will not be back."

"Nothing is guaranteed in the Cosmos," Nan said. "But yes, Falanthrow Forest is stronger." She stood with arms akimbo.

"What's this?" Corineus said. He had wandered beyond the

two-trunked tree, to where Praetor Wight had been—beating his ears nervously in the heat, looking down, tuft of hair over his brow.

They went to see. There was a mound of rich dirt in front of Corineus, about the size of a rounded garden bed. Making her way through the circle of animals, Nan stepped over to it and knelt. Bjorn winked at Bibi.

"What is it, Dad?" she whispered.

In the center of the dirt mound, a tree seedling sprouted, about as tall as Nan's thumb. Not a Falanthrow. When Bibi adjusted her glasses and squinted, it grew. Subtly, at first, in tiny, hard-to-see bursts. *Stretch. Stretch. Stretch.* But soon the bursts were bolder.

Nan looked at her husband. "What do you think of this, dear Bjorn?"

Bjorn nodded and knelt next to her, studying the seedling. He got down on his belly so he could examine it closer. "Let's see." He sat up, dug into his lab coat, and pulled out a dogeared notebook and stubby pencil. Bibi looked over his shoulder as he wrote. It looked like an equation of some sort. Next, he produced a small compass and measured the angle of the seedling.

"Just a little—this way," he said, adjusting the young tree. "There! Now it's properly aimed." He stood back up, grinning at Bibi. "The slightest miscalculation and we end up on Mars instead of Earth!"

The elk looked at one another.

Nan beamed, seeing their confusion, and scooped a little of the dark soil with her hand, lifting it, and letting it sift through her fingers. "These are the remains of Praetor Wight." She stood, pointing at the burgeoning seedling, already up to her shins. "And *that* is our way home."

Yega-Woo's black river-rock eyes shone. "I don't understand."

Bjorn crossed his arms, matter-of-factly. "Besides the benefit to your forest, destroying Praetor Wight was the key to our getting home. That's why we were in such trouble when I couldn't do it." He scratched his beard. "But when Beebs destroyed it—well, that all changed."

Bibi tilted her head. The seedling made its first leaves, each appearing with a *ping*. They framed it like the feathers of a miniature peacock. It grew so fast! She put Eek down, and the cat crept over to the young tree, warily.

"But what does Praetor Wight have to do with this tree seedling?" Bibi said.

Mom took her hand. "In the Cosmos, there are two possibilities. There is change, and there is permanence. Permanence is the only real death. That's all a zombie tree understands. But this new tree is born from change—from the ashes of Praetor Wight. An Ash tree, like the one that brought you here. This one has the power to bring us home."

Eek sat back on her haunches, watching the seedling rise over her head and up to Bibi's waist. Bjorn smiled. "Ah, we should say our goodbyes—this little tree is going to rise like a rocket soon."

"Are you going back to the other world, in the sky?" Corineus said, twitching his white tail.

"Yes," Nan said. "Will you be okay?"

"We will start again," Yega-Woo said.

Eek yowled as the sapling gave a shake and shot up several feet, until it was as tall as Bibi. The elk all took a step back. Bjorn laughed his deep laugh, wrapping an arm around one of the branches, and looking at his wife and daughter. They grabbed their own branches as Eek climbed into the tree.

"Long, happy lives to you and your forest, friends," Nan said.

Tears came back to Bibi's eyes. Would they ever see Falanthrow Forest or the elk again? She gazed at Corineus. The first friend she made here. Warmth mixed with the pins and needles, rising through her chest and lingering like a dab of wild honey on her tongue. He would be fine. The elk would be fine. She tried to put everything into a few words: "Thank you so much."

Corineus blinked his own tear-filled eyes. "Thank *you*, Bibi Blundermuss," he replied.

The sapling gave another jolt, grew up several more feet, and paused again. Bibi extended her arms overhead, still holding her branch.

The sapling appeared to flex itself—as if readying to jump into the air. Something in it rumbled. Bibi knew what *that* meant, and grasped harder, looking at her parents. They smiled: two daredevils, on the verge of an adventure.

The sapling quaked. Then: liftoff.

The elk *ooh*ed, and now the young tree began its growth spree in earnest, jerking Bibi's feet from the ground, and shooting up through the forest. With her parents, she swung her legs and climbed up. Higher and higher the tree went, pushing through the Falanthrows' still-wet branches and leaves, soaking the travelers with the cold snowmelt, as the elk grew smaller and smaller below them, calling their goodbyes.

The bees chased the tree as it rose, circling in an upward spiral, spreading out with shimmering zig-zags, like ripples on a lake.

"Thank you, Arbor Guardians," the bees buzzed in their monotone voice.

"Thank *you*, bees—we will see you again!" Nan said, as the bees split off, heading for another part of the sky—and maybe, another part of the Cosmos. The family poised on a single branch, and the brisk blue air hit their faces. Nan looked at Bjorn. "After so long, we're going home!"

"Ah, it feels good, doesn't it, *min elskede?*" he said, looking at the shrinking forest below them, and the mountains all around.

Going home. Bibi's parents held her, and her cat curled at her chest. Soon she would see Grandma Ivy . . . and sleep in her room . . . and go back to seventh grade . . . and no longer be afraid of trees. Ellery Finley would never believe it. In other words: everything would be normal.

Maybe.

Like a hand lifting them lovingly into the heavens, the giant Ash tree rose through the rest of the sky, until it escaped the blue, and pushed into the black Cosmos.

EPILOGUE

Ten months passed.

It was late, on a cold winter night. The forest next to the house had been buried in snow, and in the house, everyone slept. Everyone, that is, except Bibi, who lay side-by-side with Eek in her warm bed, staring at the ceiling.

It had been a long week—tons of homework, hanging out with new friends, helping her mom take care of the forest next to the house. But Bibi couldn't sleep. The pins and needles still tingled in her chest—but after ten months, she was used to that. Maybe it was the snow that kept her awake. It had begun that morning, without stopping since. It flitted across the rooftop, like sugar being sifted on a cake.

At least tomorrow was Saturday.

Bibi reached over to the nightstand, turning on the light.

She eyed the book she had been reading before turning in. A thirteenth birthday gift from her mom, it held deep secrets of the Arbor Guardians—their origins, their culture, their magic, their age-old war with Anaspiritus and the tree wights.

Their? Bibi smiled to herself. Ten months later, she was still getting used to thinking of herself as an Arbor Guardian, too. *Our.*

Eek stirred, eyes closed against the brightness of the nightstand light. "*Mrow,*" she squeaked, stretching her legs as far as they would go.

"Eek," Bibi said. "Do you ever wonder what will happen next? Whether more wights will come? Whether we'll meet other Arbor Guardians? Whether we'll go after Anaspiritus someday?"

Eek's eyes remained closed—her only answer a purr. Bibi sighed. Between the things her mom told her, and the things the book said, she already knew the answers. Sure, Grandma Ivy wanted the Arbor Guardian adventure to end. "It will only bring big trouble," she had said. But too late to avoid that, now.

Bibi yawned, moving her new phone out of the way so she could grab her book and prop it up with her knees. It was leather-bound, thick as a dictionary, with the title embossed in red letters:

The Way of Yggdrasil: A Compendium of Arbor Guardian Lore.
She opened it and read the first sentences out loud.

"Trees are where we come from. Without trees, there is no life. And without Arbor Guardians, there are no trees."

Eek batted her tail gently against Bibi's leg, as if trying to prod her toward sleep. "Good thing you don't have hylophobia anymore," she said, woozily.

Bibi frowned. It wasn't that simple. Hylophobia was nothing. In the Cosmos, there were way scarier things than zombie trees. She scratched Eek between the ears until the purring got louder. After a few minutes, the little black cat drifted off again.

Closing the book and putting it back on the nightstand, Bibi Blundermuss sat at the edge of the bed, and turned off the light. She moved softly to the window, pulling the curtains aside and looking up into the heavy night snow. She waited, strong and still, staring fiercely into the Cosmos.

Dear Reader:

Thank you so much for choosing this book!

You are cordially invited to leave an honest review at the online store or reader website of your choice. Reader reviews are the lifeblood of independent publishing, and your opinion is valued!

For updates on the next books in the Bibi Blundermuss series, please join the mailing list at andrewdurkinwrites.com.

Authors are nothing without readers! Thank you again.

Acknowledgments

Writing a book is hard. As I finish this one, I'm deeply grateful for numerous people whose presence immeasurably improved both the process and the resulting work.

Thank you to my agent and friend Barbara Clark. Barbara and I initially connected over my adult nonfiction, but when I announced my interest in writing fiction for kids, her first question was, "How can I help?" Her insightful and honest critique of several full *Bibi* drafts helped me find the heart of the story. Her willingness to take the manuscript on submission during the first uncertain year of the pandemic was a vote of confidence I won't soon forget.

Thank you to author, friend, and kindred spirit Emily Whitman. When I met Emily, the only thing I knew about kidlit was the list of books that changed my life as a child and that I wanted to emulate as an adult. Emily provided the inspiration, writing craft guidance, and moral support I needed to transform an earnest but vague dream into something focused and real. I'm grateful for her exquisite literary sensibility, which set a high bar that I'm still striving to reach. And I'm grateful to the many participants in her workshops, who helped me fine-tune Bibi's story in a million small but crucial ways.

Thank you to my former critique group: Christy Peterson (now a colleague at YBP), Roz Malin, Kim Kasch, Chris Clayson, and Shana Targosz. These excellent writers and friends gave me the courage to persevere through numerous setbacks and revisions. Without their camaraderie, I would likely have given up.

Thank you to Katherine Peterson for her acute and thorough proofread. She helped me see several writerly crutches that had previously escaped my notice.

Thank you to Devin Watson for his gorgeous illustrations. His gift for finding a simple expressive detail to convey the complexity of a character or scene is exactly what I try to achieve in prose. (He does it much better than I do.)

Thank you to Jeremy Solomon for bringing me on as an editor at Inkwater Press, where for five years I had the privilege of working on the manuscripts of hundreds of other authors. I'm grateful to my Inkwater colleagues: Masha Shubin, Holly Tri, Vanessa Verrill, Sean Jones, John Williams, Michael Ebert, Virginia Solan, Alan Solan, Joe Walters, Sahara Peterson, Maggie Allen, Jayme Vincent, Emily Coats, *et al.*

Thank you to my earliest beta readers—my dear friends Sharon Sekhon, Henry Caporoso, and Sarah Shute. Thank you to my middle-grade beta readers, too: Abigail Hostler and Natalie Taylor.

Most of all, thank you to Daphne and Finn, my favorite people. I have a good imagination, but I can't imagine this life without you. I love you to the end of the Cosmos and back.

Andrew Durkin
Portland, Oregon
March 2022

About the Author

Andrew Durkin (he / him) is an author, songwriter, composer, editor, student, and dreamer. He lives with his family in Oregon, where he enjoys watching trees grow and listening to the rain.

Made in the USA
Middletown, DE
16 March 2022

62698630R00142